BAREFOOT JOHN
AND
THE BLUES

EVE DUMOVICH

SNOWLINE PUBLISHING ®

Ashford, WA

First Printing, August, 2010

Although this novel is based on the history of the Pacific Northwest, it is a work of fiction and all the characters are imaginary. Many thanks to my friends, my family, T.S. Eliot, William Blake, Alfred Lord Tennyson, Matthew Arnold, Dante, Ovid and Charles Dickens.

Does she remember me? Does she hate me?
Sara rested her forehead on the cold pane. Rain streaked the
window.
She looked across the lake at the city's jagged skyline. There
were shapes in the mist and she thought she remembered music
muffled by waves.

****

In his basement office with metal grates, Philip saw a shadow
creeping, felt a spirit in the room.
There is no death without a body. There is no life without a body.
Is there?

****

Chapter One

The steam train slowed on its tracks. Salt air stung the boy's face
as he tried to see what lay behind the fog.

"Best get off here!" the engineer yelled over rattling wheels and
explosions of steam. "Next stop's up the hill at the yard! This here's
closest to where you want to go!"

The boy opened the door, swung his long body away from the
train and dropped onto marsh grass edging the dunes.

The engineer sent a short whistle burst after him. Tough times for
that kid, he thought. Tough times for everybody. The train chugged
up the hill away from the ocean.

The boy stumbled on the rocks. He looked inland where the fog was lighter. He could see an outline of a town. Smoke drifted from chimneys.

He checked his vest pocket. Grandpa Finchley's deed was still there.

"There's nothin' out there," his mother had said when his father bragged that the Finchleys were still landowners and owned six hundred acres of timberland out west. In Georgia, the family mansion had been rubble for decades and the Finchley cotton fields long gone to Northern owners.

"My Dad won that land, fair and square in a poker game," his father had replied. "Still got the deed. Sure do. And who knows what could be there? If I weren't so poorly. I'd find out. I'd take us there. We'd see."

"See Mom," the boy said as he picked his way across the slippery rocks. "There is a town here."

He sighed. He missed her. He remembered her sadness when she looked at his alcohol-soaked father.

Georgia would be steaming this time of year, he thought. Sweat would be stinging his eyes as he worked in the dust.

He would make his fortune here where it was green and cool. The Finchley name would be important again.

"They'll call me Mr. John Finchley," he said out loud. He would make Mom smile, wherever she was now.

His mother's death on his seventeenth birthday had not made him angry. He knew it was her time to go. He knew it was his time to claim his inheritance six months later, after his father finished drinking himself to death.

As soon as his father's funeral was over, John had taken the deed to the town's attorney, got more documents proving that he was the rightful heir to the lands described in the deed, and climbed aboard a freight train heading west.

The Depression gripped the country. It was hard to find food and shelter but he kept on moving, moving on across desert and mountains to the Pacific Ocean.

As sandpipers scurried ahead of him, the mist cleared and he saw a white cliff, tufted with green, rising in vast steps above the churning sea.

There, up there, he would build his house – a big house, a mansion.

Wind whistled in the gnarled firs. Drift logs rolled and beat against the rocks. He stopped and looked at a crow winging through sullen clouds. It would soon be dark.

He moved quickly along the beach to the buildings ahead.

He slept that night under the pilings at the end of Main Street. At daybreak, he presented himself at a wooden shack with a sign that read "Abraham Logging."

"I can log. I can do anything," he told the man behind the desk.

Oley Sorgenson looked at John appraisingly, taking in his lanky frame and the wiry strength of his arms and back. The boy looked like he had been doing some hard work. Oley nodded and handed him some papers to sign.

"You're on," Oley said. "The crummy's leavin' 'bout now."

"The crummy?"

"The crew truck. Behind the building."

John joined the men in the truck for a bumpy ride over potholes and rocks. The truck headed uphill around switchbacks and boulders until it stopped where trees waited for felling.

The crew chief showed him how to set chokers, the heavy cables fastened to downed trees after their branches had been removed, and told him where to start. John scrambled over jagged tree trunks and piles of branches, set the chokers and watched the massive logs pulled by an engine called the steam donkey up the mountainside to the railway tracks.

He soon realized how dangerous his job could be; thousand-pound logs rolled easily and the cables sometimes snapped.

John learned quickly and was soon promoted to the "misery whip," a long cross-cut saw powered by human muscle. John felled and rigged and hauled. His arms and back filled out. By season's end and the first snowfall, his coworkers were calling him "Big John" to distinguish him from other loggers called John.

"That kid is one hard worker but tight as a tick," they said because Big John never joined them in the tavern for beer or played cards or tried to impress any of the women.

Big John spent his money on boots, work clothes and mail-order books about keeping accounts. He studied the Doyle, Scribner and International log rules that explained how to estimate the board feet of timber and the actual amount of marketable wood in any given tree. With Oley's help, he practiced the math involved. Big John paid for his room and board at "Miss Sally's" rooming house and put the rest of his pay in the bank. When the snow was too deep for logging, he worked in the office helping Oley with paperwork.

Oley, who had no family of his own, ran the Abraham Logging Company office for a Portland-based corporation. He enjoyed teaching John what he knew. John told Oley about his grandfather's deed so Oley introduced John to the Abraham Logging Company lawyer who helped file the documents needed to claim the Finchley acres.

Apart from Oley, Big John did not make many friends, although he had no enemies either. He never seemed to smile, which made people uneasy.

Big John also never scowled or fought. He stared down his challengers. They were diverted from their desire to hit him by the strange expression in his dark eyes.

"Shit. He's not even ornery. He's an odd one," the other loggers said. "But he sure is a worker."

In a few seasons, John Finchley saved enough money to buy the equipment he needed to begin logging his land. He hired a crew and started his own mill.

In 1936, Big John Finchley was one of the first to buy the new gasoline-powered chainsaws. After that, Finchley trees fell faster and traveled farther. As Oregon became the leading timber producer in the country, Big John bought more land and more stock in the railroad.

The town of Abraham thrived and spread around the Finchley mill, railroad yard and depot.

By 1940, Big John Finchley was rich, just as he had dreamed he would be.

"He's still a sour cuss," the townspeople reminded each other.

Big John's stubborn, single-minded approach to life and his inability to smile etched grooves around his mouth. His eyes were expressionless most of the time, although occasionally a child's laugh or the sight of a puppy seemed to make him look a little confused, as if he were missing something.

Finchley timber rode the rails down the coast and to the wood-starved cities. The mills further inland were running out of logs as houses and roads overran the forest. Big John bought shares in foundries and acquired more timberland.

The Finchley mills bustled. Their board feet brought dollars to the little town, where whales still battled in the surf and constant rain kept trees strong, straight and dark green.

Finchley trees turned into houses and paper for the hordes of people pushing their way west from east coast cities shaded by skyscrapers.

Finchley Logging boomed during World War II and, after the war ended, became even more prosperous as cities and towns spread with ever-increasing populations. Big John's trips up and down the west coast made him wonder if California would soon be too crowded. He also wondered what the smoke from all the new automobiles would do if it stayed trapped in the Pacific fog for many years.

"I bet in few years, they won't be able to see the stars. Those orange trees will die out," he told Oley, now manager of the Finchley Logging office in Abraham.

"Them Californians!" Oley sniffed. "They'll want to move up here then."

Big John looked thoughtful and proceeded to buy thousands of acres of land along the Oregon coast.

A few months later, as he rode a train home from a visit to his Portland law firm of Rolled, Smythe and Right, it occurred to him that time was passing as fast as the trees hurtling past his window.

Soon, he would be too old to create someone to carry on the family name. It was time to breed. He must have children to protect his land. The Finchley family must not end with him.

Children? He scratched his chin. The problem was he had never been fond of children. Breeding was breeding, all the same. He could satisfy himself as easily with a wife as he could with the girls in Portland's dance halls. His wife would breed. His mind chugged along with the rhythm of the wheels. Even if there was another war or the harsh and windy coast was covered by smoke and fog, his son could move on and keep the line going, as he had done. Even if his son woke up in the morning with nothing to lose, looking for his walking shoes, he could move on – perhaps to find another stretch of sand.

It was time to find a wife. Good stock was important.

It shouldn't be hard to find someone, he thought. Women were always trying to interest him by playing up their small size, their need for a big man and by being soft and gentle. While it was fun to bed them, he did not want a small, soft and gentle woman as a wife. Southern weak and dependent women had helped destroy his family and its power. Their blood was thin. What he needed was a woman as strong as his timber.

The next Sunday, much to the surprise of all the women in Abraham, Big John Finchley attended the Methodist Church. He had decided to pick his bride-to-be from the females handing out baked goods during the coffee hour.

"Praise the Lord," the women said, happy to see him in church.

The men knew better. The few who worked closely with him and had spoken with him, understood what he was looking for.

"Damn odd way to find a woman," his foreman, Slick, commented.

"I suppose it's one way to find a good wife," Andy, the high rigger, replied.

"Good way to get a dull one," Slick said.

Tall, wide and serious Janice Brown caught John's eye. She looked calm and capable as she passed the cookies and filled the cups. John remembered someone saying that she was a good gardener and knew how to save money.

He asked Slick to introduce him to the family.

"Poor girl," Slick muttered, but did as he was asked.

John Finchley said "How-de-do Ma'am" to tiny and wiry Ida Brown and shook the callused hand of Sam Brown. Daughter Janice bobbed awkwardly, bending her neck like a horse to the plow. John noted her wide hips and sturdy stance.

He did not notice the sad darkness in her eyes and that she was not quite aware of where she was.

"Why'd he pick that one?" Debbie, Slick's wife, asked her friend, Sandy. "She's a might strange. Her sister Audrey's prettier and has more git up and go."

"Good thing, though," Sandy replied. "Audrey's stuck on Gary Smith."

"Really? That guitar-pickin' fool?"

Sandy handed Debbie a lemon square and the conversation lapsed.

****

John was invited to Sunday dinner at the Browns that evening. He had spent the afternoon checking some newly fallen timber and was still wearing his caulk boots, the leather, nail-soled boots the men called corks. He took them off at the door. Ida never let men wear corks in the house, not even if there was an emergency.

John became a regular visitor. He was impressed by the clean house and the simple cooking. After dinner, he sat with Janice on the porch swing. She spoke when she was spoken to and never volunteered anything. John liked her silence. She would do as she was bid and she was strong. He could see that.

One evening, when he came to eat, John noticed that Ida was nervous, fluttering around the kitchen like a trapped bird. She said Sam had not made it home yet.

"He's not one to be late for a meal," she said.

"He could have been delayed in the woods," John suggested.

"Maybe," Ida replied, sounding doubtful.

They waited for another half hour and then ate without Sam's presence. Ida frowned and her hands shook.

Afterwards, while John and Janice rocked on the swing in the fading light, they heard cries and shouts from the road below. A strange procession wound its way through the shadows until it reached the porch.

John and Janice sprang to their feet. Janice's mouth opened. She gasped and stayed with her mouth frozen open. John inhaled and swore.

Slick was the lead bearer. His hands were cupped behind him keeping two planks and their burden on an even keel. Behind him, stretched out face upward on the makeshift stretcher, lay Sam. Sam's eyes were open and surprised. His body seemed to have been compressed to half its normal size and oozed blood and tissue. His legs dangled on either side of the planks. His corks made red trails in the dust.

"A spar, a rogue spar. He never saw it coming," Slick said.

Ida came to the doorway and held up her hand. It shook. They understood. They put their burden down and took off their boots. By the time they had done that and picked the planks up again, Ida had cleared the dinner dishes. They laid Sam out on the kitchen table. There was blood on the floor but nobody tracked in any mud.

They buried Sam in the Methodist churchyard. Everybody in town attended the wake at the Abraham Tavern. They remembered him with beer, stories and pretzels. His was not the first wake that year. Nor would it be the last. Grizzled faces moistened and women sniffed away sobs. So it went.

After giving the girls and their mother a week to mourn, John resumed his visits to the Brown house to see Janice. He noticed that after the funeral, Ida seemed to fade. She was as clean and as neat as ever but walked silently through the days. She spent the evenings rocking by the stove, looking sadly at Sam's corks still warming on the hearth.

"We should get married soon," John told Janice after two more weeks had passed.

Janice nodded.

Sister Audrey was glad to have something else to think about. Audrey said she'd do all the planning since Ida was not up to it.

As Ida rocked, Audrey helped Janice sew her wedding gown.

****

Although the Methodist Church hall was small, there was plenty of room for the few guests invited to the ceremony since John had no family and few friends. Only Ida's and Sam's cousins and some of John's key employees heard the marriage vows mumbled by the stiff-backed couple.

In contrast, the reception in the Grange Hall was attended by most of the town's residents. Good parties were hard to come by. Gary Smith and his guitar led the band that included Slim Jim on the fiddle, Ivan Idunovich on the accordion, Sven Swede on the washboard, Luke Lindstrom on the jug and old Pete Hjorstad on the washtub base.

Around the hall, tables groaned with white fluffy cakes, jars of pickled kelp, elk meatballs in chanterelle sauce and slices of bear sausage. Applejack and keg beer flowed.

John looked puzzled by the enthusiasm of the crowd as he and Janice made their entrance but he seemed gratified. He knew what was expected of him, however, so he started the party by dancing with his equally awkward bride.

When Janice threw her bouquet into the crowd, Sandy caught it by mistake. She was already married to Mitch and was certainly no virgin. She tossed it quickly to Audrey, who was standing by the bandstand, giggling.

John and Janice then left the hall. They sat silently in the front seat of John's black Packard as he drove it up the dirt road away from town to his big house on the cliff.

After they were gone, Ida asked Audrey to take her home.

"I need to sit by the stove," Ida said. Audrey understood her mother didn't want to be too far from Sam's corks.

Once Ida was settled, she looked up at her youngest daughter.

"You did good, girl," she told Audrey. "It's your turn next."

Audrey looked at her mother sadly. Gary had already asked her to marry him but she did not want to leave her mother alone.

"One wedding at a time," she said, shaking her head.

"I know you're worried about me," Ida went on. "But it would make me happy to see you happy. I know your Pa would like it."

****

Audrey and Gary were married a month later. Their wedding reception rattled the rafters as the young couple whirled around the room in the foot-stompin' logger's polka. Boots drummed on the cedar planks and skirts billowed like hemlocks in a high wind.

The sounds floated up the hill road to Ida as she rocked back and forth in the porch swing. She heard the distant accordion wail, the thud of the boots, the wind in the trees and the swing creaking under a starless sky.

Now both girls are taken care of, she thought. Old Sam is waitin' on me. He probably hasn't changed his socks since he passed beyond.

Her head bent low as she slipped away to join him while corks thumped and the fiddle played.

Sandy stopped by the house the next morning and found her slumped over, looking, as Sandy later said, as if she was just taking a nap.

Sandy picked up the old lady, took her inside and carefully laid her out on the bed before walking to the tavern to ask Mitch to fetch the newlyweds from Gary's cabin.

****

Audrey thought the next few days were too bright and too sad at the same time. She missed her mother and could not stop her tears when she thought of her. At the same time, Gary was everything she had dreamed of in a husband. He held her, encouraged her and loved her.

Ida had planned ahead. Her dresser drawer contained a neatly written note, enclosed in a white envelope marked, "In the event of my death." The note asked that she be buried in the family plot beside Sam because the plot was bought and paid for, as was her headstone. It was to be inscribed simply with her name, her dates and the words "Wife and Mother" and no "fancy stuff."

The note also enclosed instructions for Audrey and Janice to report to Bob Frendham, president of the Bank of Abraham. He had the will and was in charge of the savings account. Each daughter was to take half of the money in the bank, sell the house and split the profits. It seemed that Ida's frugality had paid off. The savings account came to just over $10,000.

"You don't have to log no more!" Audrey told Gary. "We can set up that hardware store you always wanted!"

"I can't take your money," Gary said.

Audrey burst into tears.

"You don't like logging!" she cried. "And it can kill you! Look what happened to Pa! And the others! I couldn't stand it if I lost you! Besides it's our money! Momma would have wanted it that way!"

Gary knew she was right. He bought an abandoned house near the center of town and turned it into a hardware store. It carried garden tools, automotive parts and other items not sold in the Abraham General Store.

****

John was happy to take Janice's share. He invested it in steel and coal. Janice did not seem to care what he did with it. However, John had been impressed by Ida's forethought so he went to Portland to ask his lawyers to redraft his will so that his sons could split the estate evenly.

"Fair's fair," he said. "They should get equal shares."

"I thought you just got married," commented his attorney, Benjamin Rolled. "You got kids somewhere else?"

John shook his head.

"Not at all. But I will have sons very soon."

"No daughters?"

John shrugged.

"I hope not," he said. "I'll worry about that when it happens."

He went home and began to work on creating the next generation of Finchleys.

****

Janice was submissive to the state of their union. She plodded through her married life with the quiet endurance that made people refer to her as a "good" woman.

But she was not happy. She had never learned to express the strange dreams and the thoughts that whispered in her mind and that sent pain through her heart. She missed her home and her family. She missed hearing Audrey laugh and her mother scold.

Now, alone in the big house on the cliff, she only found peace when she stood by her open bedroom window, listening to the thundering surf; feeling the dark roar of the water and the singing of the trees deep in her bones.

Her mind rode the wind and the waves like the seagulls on a stormy day. Within her blood grew a restlessness she never gave a name to, never told about, never shared. Her blood rose with the rhythm of the moon and sank with the waning tide.

Like the tall, wind-bent trees, she bore the buffeting of her inner storm. She bore her unceasing loneliness. She bore the calm and businesslike administrations of her husband, who had determined she would – she must – bear him a son because that was her job.

He had estimated her worth correctly. She was pregnant within six months of their wedding.

"Oh you lucky thing!" Audrey cried.

Janice bowed her head.

Audrey stared at her sister.

"Aren't you happy? I'd be delighted. Gary and I keep trying and trying. But nothing has happened so far."

"Happy?" Janice twisted her hands into her apron. "Not, not – "
She saw the distress on her sister's face.

"But not unhappy," Janice said quickly. "Not really."

Audrey crossed the room and hugged her.

She would never understand her sister. Janice was always sweet and kind but often Audrey felt she knew only a small piece of her, a little surface piece. Sometimes, her sister was so shielded that Audrey could not ask, would not dare to ask, what was really wrong.

Ida had once explained that Janice was a little "touched."

When Audrey asked, "What touched her?" Ida replied, "Perhaps an angel or the wind."

Whatever had touched her then was surely grabbing her now, Audrey mused as she held her sister's trembling body and stroked away the fear.

Why is she so afraid? What is she afraid of?

Audrey didn't know. Janice couldn't say.

Nobody knew.

Big John did not know. He had noticed that his wife seemed to become more and more unhappy as fall blanketed the house and her body thickened and swelled. She stopped speaking and stared into the darkness outside.

He noticed but decided it was not his business. She was doing her job and her time of deliverance would come.

****

It did come, finally, as a gale pushed the ocean waves into foaming peaks and driving, biting rain, blown sideways in a bitter wind, lashed the land. On that night, Janice found deliverance.

Audrey and the midwife listened to the keening outside the rafters as Janice writhed in agony. Big John sat alone in the living room below, wondering why he felt so desolate.

"She ain't strong," the midwife said.

"Oh, try. Just try," Audrey begged her sister.

It seemed that as the child in Janice had quickened so her own life had diminished. It was as if this child was the ground in which she planted her whole soul, her dreams, her hopes and her pain. Once he was born, she had no need to live.

Audrey knew her sister was dying as she cuddled her small, squalling nephew and the midwife battled for Janice's life.

"She's all in you," Audrey whispered to Little John as he wept.

Audrey understood that this baby held all the songs his mother had never allowed herself to sing, all the colors she never saw and all the words she never spoke. As Janice's seed breathed free of the husk of her body, her soul sprung from its dark, storm-tossed container and flew off into the driving wind. Janice Finchley was no more.

Audrey took care of Little John for the first few weeks of his life until his father shipped a trained nurse from Portland to do the job. Then Audrey returned to her home and husband, Gary, who had missed her.

"Time we got one of our own," Gary said.

But Audrey was never to bear a child, no matter how hard they tried to start a baby between them.

****

Meanwhile, Little John grew. He was as unlike his father as day was from night. As soon as he could speak, he asked questions for which there were no answers. He loved the music he heard on the radio, the drums, the strings and the trumpets. He loved little glittery things and picked agates from the beach with his Aunt Audrey. He loved soft feathers that floated from the sky. He saw flowing hair and horses in the white clouds that puffed above the sea on a sunny spring day.

Aunt Audrey wondered what lay before the boy.

When Little John was born, a storm at sea blew away his mother's soul, Audrey recalled. He had already experienced loss and loneliness. The world had been infected by prejudice, holocaust, genocide, and the atom bomb. Would it heal before he had to go into it on his own?

When Little John came to visit, Gary played his guitar and taught him songs to sing with him.

Little John's favorite was Jimmy Kennedy's version of "The Teddy Bears' Picnic."

"If you go down in the woods today, you're sure of a big surprise! If you go down in the woods today, you'd better go in disguise!"

Audrey thought it strange how much Little John took to music.

"He didn't get it from his father, that's for sure," she told Gary.

"That man don't give a hoot for nothin' but money," Gary replied.

****

Big John tried to care but he knew nothing about children. His own childhood had been so long ago. He remembered it only as a collection of vague forms; shadowy figures who were once his parents and others he once knew but whose names he had forgotten, and who had vanished into a world long gone.

When he thought about Janice, it seemed that a cold wind blew. Still, she had given him a son. But it was hard to understand this tiny creature. Children are a different species, he decided. It was easier to concentrate on business, to think about ways to make sure that his son and his son's sons would never want for anything.

When Little John turned five, the Portland nurse came to Big John and told him that she was leaving.

"He don't need a nurse no more," the nurse said. "I got another job in Portland, where there are more people. I'm going tomorrow."

Big John blinked vaguely and wandered into the kitchen where Sandy, who had been his housekeeper since Janice died, was cooking dinner.

"The nurse is going," Big John said. "Can you look out for the boy while I'm at work? He can still stay at his aunt's on your days off and when I'm out of town."

"Sure thing," Sandy uttered as she stirred dumpling dough.

Sandy fed Little John him each morning, set out a sandwich at lunch time and washed his hands and face before his father came home for dinner. When she didn't see him, she decided the boy was at his Aunt Audrey's, which was fine with her because the child was sort of strange and she wasn't sure what to do with him.

At first, Little John amused himself making shapes out of twigs and stones in the weed-covered backyard. At dinner, he faced his father at the end of the long dark table while his father read the newspaper and ate. After dinner, Little John took himself to bed. He took off his clothes and brushed his teeth as the nurse had taught him.

As the weather warmed up, Little John stopped wearing shoes because they were too much trouble to tie up. Sandy called him "that barefoot boy" when she met Mitch and their friends at the Abraham Tavern.

Barefoot, Little John grew stronger leaning against the wind. He left the backyard and walked down to the beach. He felt sand between his toes and the soles of his feet became leather-tough from running over the barnacles. His fingers became nimble and strong as he pulled seaweed from the sand and burst its air-filled pockets. He liked the sound and thought they popped better when they were dry.

He spent most of his time on the shore, unless he went to visit Aunt Audrey. On rainy days, she fed him tea and oranges that came all the way from China. Some sunny days she took him with her as she hunted for agates and the sea-blue Japanese fishnet floats that came in with the high tide. Other days he wandered alone along the water's edge.

One morning, he traveled a little further than usual. He saw a strange silhouette against the shoreline.

What was that? Who was that?

He had seen Garbage Can Red.

****

Garbage Can Red, called "Can" for short by the locals, lived in an old fishing boat stranded on a dune. Can had a long white beard and long white hair. Each morning before the sun turned the beach silver, he walked through Abraham and selected what he needed from the garbage cans people left propped beside their shake-shingled houses.

"Take never no mind," they said. "He never harms nothin'."

They said he'd once been a fisherman but one night storm waves tossed him and his boat ashore and he hit his head. When he woke up, they said, he'd gone funny and couldn't tell anybody who he was or where he'd come from. So Can and his boat stayed where they were, depending, at all times, on the kindness of strangers who left a little extra food on their back porches for the harmless and lonely old man, whose eyes were like the sea shrouded by fog and whose back bent like a wind-whipped fir.

That hot summer morning, Can shuffled out of the wooden door of his tilted boat, slung an empty burlap sack over his shoulder and moved carefully down a rope ladder to where sand had climbed the keel to form a sloping, granular ramp. His knuckles tightened on the rope once he reached the beach. He leaned his head against the boat to get his bearings and to remind himself of his intentions.

"Hi!" came a shrill voice from low down, somewhere behind him.

Was them come to get him? Can wondered.

"Eh!" he ejaculated and turned his beard slowly in the direction of the sound. He let one hand go until his back was pressed on the planks. "Eh?"

The small creature squatting on the sand gazed at him gravely, bright brown eyes serious, rose-pink mouth pouting. Black hair surrounded a round moon face with astonishingly dark eyebrows for something so small. It extended one short arm and pointed one tiny finger at the now confused and slightly uneasy Can.

"Your house?"

Can surveyed the imperious midget and decided this one was too short to get him.

"Eh?" Can said.

"Can I see?" it asked.

Can frowned. There was something different about this morning. Nobody had ever spoken to him like that. It didn't matter. He had to go to town and look in the cans. He had to do that every morning. This was morning. This was important. This midget could not stop him.

"I have to go to town," Can announced.

The squatting figure put its arm down. It nodded understandingly. "Me too," it announced.

Can shrugged and moved away from the boat towards the first road that ended on the beach.

After a few steps, he felt small fingers slipping into his palm. His own rough digits closed gently around the little hand placed so trustingly in his.

Together, Can and Little John shuffled through the blown sand, up to the asphalt, to the main road and down the alleys behind the houses. The tall, stooped and bearded wanderer and the small dark-haired boy, hand-in-hand, looked through cans and found sweetness in the strangest places.

The rain took a vacation that summer and the usual lumbering gray clouds disappeared. For a few weeks, the sun baked the sand and turned the agates into jewels.

Little John and Can befriended new cats and old dogs and collected sticks and rocks. After each day of scrounging, they sat back against the weather-beaten planks of the boat and stared out at the rocking sea, saying little as they breathed bright salt air.

"Eh," Can would comment from time to time.

"Yup," Little John would say, nodding agreement.

****

Audrey was happy and busy, combing the beach below the cliffs for agates. Gary was setting them into a walkway and slicing them up for a new fireplace. She loved the way the agates would tell their multi-colored stories and the way their colors shaped into trees, skies, mountains and whirling planets in gold, brown, red, orange, yellow and silver white.

Audrey wondered why Little John stopped visiting her and why he was never at her end of the beach. She thought maybe that Sandy was taking the boy somewhere. Audrey didn't feel right asking Big John about his son because they rarely spoke and she was sure he would tell her it was none of her business. In any case, Gary didn't like his brother-in-law so he wouldn't want her to go visiting.

Little John is almost six by now anyway, Audrey thought. Maybe his dad is finally paying some attention to him. That would be good.

Audrey tried to stop worrying about her nephew as she selected the stones that showed their colors only when they were wet or polished.

****

Big John spent most of that summer up the coast at the town of Forks working out ways to bring its lumber to his mill. More and more people needed wood to build houses and factories.

Forks was booming. Its mills were too busy to handle all the trees felled on the banks of the Hoh River, around La Push and up Puget Sound. Big John was not home to see that Little John was never home during the day. Thoughts of his small son never crossed his mind, filled as it was with numbers, board feet and sawdust.

****

Little John ran home at the end of each day with Can as dusk turned the sea pink. Sandy always left supper on the table for the scrubby, scraggly boy, for whom, she told Mitch, she felt mighty sorry, mighty sorry indeed.

Mitch was almost as big as Sandy, but while her size lay broadside of her hips, his bulk swayed across his massive stomach, stuffed and rounded by gravy, grease and drink. Mitch worked his shift at the mill and at the end of each day, washed the sawdust from his teeth with beer at the tavern which smelled of cedar and oil and sweat. There, the men perched along the dark-wooden bar on round wooden stools, suspenders stretched against buttons and corks propped on the brass rail.

"She makes sure he's fed," Mitch said as foam whitened the stubble above his lip. "But he jest runs wild, like a cat."

"Or a coyote," Beaner said. He was a smallish man with deep-sunk black eyes and hair that sprouted from his head in jagged clumps.

"Yep. He'll be trouble," mid-sized Salty agreed.

Salty scratched his crotch. Salty was always scratching something. He sweated profusely, even during cold weather. Red blotches spread across his hairless, blimp-like face.

Angie, the bartender, nodded sagely and stored another bit of information she would share with any patron who needed conversation. Angie paid attention to everything she heard in the Abraham Tavern. Angie knew that her power lay in knowing just about everything about everybody and spreading it around.

Gossip was the glue that held the community of loggers, mill workers, storekeepers and housewives together. Gossip flowed from the tavern, to the church, down the street and around dinner tables. Like the rain flowing through gutters, it drew force, changed shape and gathered power. Its facts took on another dimension and brought all its participants down to the same level of ignorance and up to the same level of excitement. Some truth was in it when it started but it flowed so fast that the truth could not catch up and finally was left behind entirely.

That summer, it caught up with Little John and Can. The town of Abraham stirred and noticed the boy and his companion.

Until now, they said, nobody had been bothered by Can. They were used to him, used to his ways. He never did nobody no harm, they said. Leastways, none you could tell. But what was he doing with the kid?

Mitch told Sandy what folks were saying. Sandy bit her lower lip. It wasn't her fault. She was just housekeeping. She wasn't hired as babysitter. Anyhow, that kid never minded her. He needed his father. His father should look out for the lad, give him some discipline. She thought of talking to Big John when he came back from Forks but she was afraid. Big John could be a mite tetchy and she might lose her job with him.

Her friends tried to help out. They were genuinely concerned about Little John and tried to lure him away from Can.

They would wait and call to the boy when they saw him burrowing in a garbage can or routing under a bush. They thought he would be drawn by cookies, milk and a kind smile. He was, to a point. He would eat the cookies, drink the milk and then as soon as he could, they said, he'd "high-tail it out the door and back to that Can."

They did not understand that the lonely child, with an old spirit, and a lonely man, with the mind of child, had become best friends. The pair enjoyed the sun and the sunsets. They spoke very little but they understood each other.

Most of the speaking in Abraham that summer was by its other residents who, despite their kind hearts, watched everybody with blinkered eyes and worried about everything they did not understand. They thought words and righteous indignation would

give them some control over the world in which they lived and
provide some shelter from the gathering storm.

Chapter Two

Abraham straddled the coast highway before it tunneled between Douglas firs, crept along the cliff and wound down through a field of salt-gray marsh grass. Then it cut inland, crossed the Cascade mountains and joined the highway to Portland.

The first building at the south end of Abraham was a three-story cedar shake house, with a steeped roof, a white fence and square front yard. This was the Stone residence. The Stones were among the first families to settle Abraham. Many believed the Stones would be among the last.

"A Stone is a Stone. You know," the locals said.

The Stones owned more land than Big John and they had held it longer. They had built Abraham's Methodist Church, the school and donated land for the cemetery. They owned Abraham General Store and sold gasoline from the only pump in town.

While Can and Little John were sharing their days wandering together, there were three living Stones; old Matthew, his daughter Katy and her daughter, Sara.

Matthew Stone was more than six feet tall and stick thin. His nose seemed too heavy for his height so it pulled his face forward and bent his neck. Everything was too far beneath that nose. It forced the bushy eyebrows above it to pull in and the bright red mouth below to push out and purse with permanent disapproval.

Matthew Stone had always been tight and narrow. When he was nineteen, after his father and mother died of influenza, Matthew decided it was time to start replenishing the Stone stock. Matthew, like Big John, believed in good blood from a good breed and selected fourteen-year-old Melissa Osborne from Portland as the vessel for his personal multiplication.

The Osbornes were an established but ambitious family and were happy to trade their daughter for some good timberland.

Placid Melissa, who had been raised in a carefully monitored atmosphere of gentility and graciousness, was as obedient as she was misinformed. Her mind was stuffed with the fictionalized joys of wifehood so she went blissfully to her destiny.

But Melissa did not thrive once transplanted to the wilder part of the Pacific Coast. Her energy lasted only long enough to produce little Katy Stone. Then Melissa faded fast in the shadow of her husband's bitter disappointment that she had not given him a son. She seemed unable to bear fruit again, no matter how many times he plowed in his seed.

Barely twenty, Melissa drifted into a fog of woe and whisky. Her thick brown hair grew lank as her body spread, flattened by the weight of her life. The luster in her eyes faded to opaque misery. Matthew found her undesirable. He decided that sober little Katy was Stone enough so he spent his evenings either playing checkers with other businessmen in Abraham or visiting the unmarried but accessible waitress at the Abraham Diner, who liked him and his presents.

Ignored by the townsfolk, who disapproved of her drinking but did not want to anger old Matthew, Melissa stumbled daily from her white house to the depot where she sat on a bench to tip her flask into her mouth and watch the trains steam away from town.

A railroad worker in town to fix the tracks saw her there one day. He joined her during his break and then again on several days following. After a while, they began to meet after dark because he found her to be a willing partner, easily sharing her bottle and her body.

"Come away with me," he whispered one dark and lusty night. "My job's done. I got to go."

"Sure," she mumbled.

They hopped a freight before dawn. Melissa never looked back. She was not missed and was never heard from again.

****

For a few years, Katy wondered about her mother. But by the time she was eighteen, Katy had forgotten what Melissa looked like and did not think about her at all.

Matthew never remarried. He ran the store until Katy was old enough to take over. Then he spent his time playing checkers on the porch while Katy ran the business. Katy worked hard. She was pure Stone.

Katy was already selling Stone goods when Big John Finchley married Janice and fathered Little John. This marriage was a disappointment to Katy. She had been eyeing Big John for some time.

That John Finchley messed up, Kathy thought as she poured beans into a barrel. That Janice is a weird one and she's got that flighty sister, Audrey. Now if he'd married me, that would have been a much better business.

However, Katy was not one for crying over spilled milk so she set her sights on Lars Gustavsen who was a regular customer.

Lars is not that bright, Kathy thought. But he'll be easy to manage, has large bones and can give the Stone family more strength. He will father a big boy.

It took only four months for Katy to talk Lars into marrying her.

"It's like a mountain lion marryin' a 'possum," Sandy whispered to Mitch as they sat in the back of the Methodist Church during the wedding.

"She's a tad sharp for my taste," her husband whispered back.

Katy was impregnated on her honeymoon, which was only for one night because Lars had to get back to work.

Katy barely noticed her condition. She kept working until her contractions began. Then she walked over to Mary the midwife's house, where without pain, and with great determination, Katy pushed out a tiny, mewling, blue-eyed baby girl.

"A girl! You're kidding!" Katy cried when Mary handed her the bundle. "Damn!"

Katy named her frail offspring Sara, hoping some Biblical strength might toughen the miserably small baby.

She breastfed Sara just long enough to find a milk goat, then left the baby and the goat in the care of Milly, Matthew Stone's housekeeper.

Katy did not give up her dream of bearing a son but her desire for Lars' attentions was such a strange combination of persistence and indifference, Lars became confused.

Did she love him? Did he love her? He didn't know. But it didn't feel right. He was tired at night and she would never leave him alone.

His loins made the decision for the both of them. He came home only to sleep. Katy knew he would never father a son with her. Months passed. Years passed.

****

Katy's mouth shrunk into a small replica of her father's tight lips. Her eyes hardened and sarcasm drove all sweetness from her tone. Her granite words chipped away at her husband's spirit and drive.

On the job, Lars began to stumble. He wasn't thinking, couldn't think, until one day he fell off a log that rolled and crushed the life from him.

So Katy and Sara moved back to the big Stone house, where Milly continued to watch over the little girl who cried too much and caught too many colds.

"Puny," grumbled Katy as she stacked cans.

By then, Matthew Stone's age hung over him like a shroud. His nose had dragged his back so low that he walked bent over like a fishing pole with its hook caught in a log. He spent his days hooked by the checker table on the store's front porch.

Katy, surrounded by cans, beans, flour, saws, rope, tarps, dog biscuits, canned soup, cloth, canvas, fishing tackle and lines, loved the stacks of useful items that towered around. She knew to the cent, to the inch, to the ounce and to the pound, what came and what went out; who paid what, what was owed and by whom. It was said that she had an account book for a brain.

"It's clear that woman has no heart. You can tell by the way her kid cries all the time. You know she never holds that baby," Milly told her husband, Beaner.

"That baby's too young to know her Mom's the queen of the general store," Beaner said drily. "That woman cares more about cans and yard goods."

From dawn to dusk, Katy perched on her stool like a hooded owl, her eyes half shut against the gray light slanting through the dusty windows. The blackened counter was her defense against customers who might try to waste her time on idle chatter, who were not serious about the value of the cans, the feed or the dried beans they needed.

John Finchley saw Katy on her perch many times. He noticed her granite bearing, admired her business-like aura, her lowered eyes and the axe-sharp line of her jaw.

However, until one hot August morning as crows took their positions along the electric wire across from the store, he had not thought of addressing her beyond the basic exchanges of dollars and cents, weights and measures.

That morning, Mitch blocked Big John's passage down the boardwalk along Main Street.

Stopped by a mill worker! In front of the Stone store! And for what reason?

Mitch's widespread person forced Big John Finchley to stop walking because there was no way around him without stepping into the gutter.

"Ahhh!" Mitch said ominously.

The astonished Big John Finchley looked at the broad, red face below him. Finchley's eyebrows coalesced. He stared down at the impediment to his passage.

Mitch was not impressed. He did not move. Mitch had never liked Finchley. Mitch was glad Sandy made a few dollars working for him but Mitch thought Finchley was way too uppety for a guy who hadn't even been born and raised in Abraham.

"He might be rich – but so what?" Mitch told his friends in the tavern. "There's more to a man than money."

Now he had something on that Big John Finchley. He had something on him that proved no matter how much money that man had, he was no better than anyone else. Perhaps worse. He was not taking care of his kid. So Mitch felt right about using a surly tone, taking a belligerent stance because Mitch had to SAY something. What's right was right.

"So whatcha gonna do 'bout that kid?" Mitch growled.

Finchley's eyes held a hint of confusion.

"Excuse me?" he asked.

"That kid of yourn," Mitch said. "My Sandy said he keeps runnin' off and she cain't track him 'cause she has to stay at yer place and clean. My Sandy said she thought the kid was jes' goin' to his aunt's. And here's he's been hanging out with that beach-livin' loony and pickin' through garbage cans for food."

"What?" Finchley was astounded.

"That's right," Mitch went on. "Everybody seen him. That kid of your'n, pickin' garbage for food. Don't seem right. Thought you oughta know."

Mitch finished this last with the smugness only felt by those who have corrected a social wrong. He stepped aside.

Finchley, his courage failing, could now move forward. However, he needed a refuge so he moved left, strode past the checker players on the porch and hurried inside where he met the implacable stare of Queen Katy.

She had heard every word. She had seen Finchley's humiliation and she knew that he had been brought down to size by his small and wandering son.

Katy thought of her perfectly controlled Sara and looked up at Big John.

Her hard glitter gaze met his confused stare. They both knew then that something else was happening then, although neither would normally shape their lips around the word, neither would usually allow a thought of such linkage clutter their mind. But there it was, glowing between them like phosphorous in a deep and waveless bay.

They had met before, had done business before but never before had this strange darkness wrapped them in its space.

"I'd like," he murmured, held fast by the moment.

"You'd like what?" she demanded unblinking.

"I'd like some more fishin' line," he blurted.

"Usual?" she asked.

Her blue eyes gleamed. The strands of hair that sprung from the bun clamped at the back of her neck were like wire. Her cheeks were sharp crags above her determined lips. He was suddenly aware that she smelled of soap and dust.

He nodded.

She tilted her head and looked at him with a sudden onslaught of speculation. He had just been humiliated. She cast her own fishing line. The time was right.

"Say," she said. She allowed a faint smile to soften the edge of her lips.

He looked at her in silence. Something made him cautious. The less you said, the less likely to give offense, he thought.

"I heard 'bout the kid," she said.

He remained quiet. His eyebrows grew more tightly together. She felt the air around him thicken.

She put sympathy upon her face.

"It's no easy thing to raise a kid on your own," she added.

He nodded warily.

Katy pulled the fishing line from the reel.

"Same amount?" she asked.

He nodded again.

As she drew the line from the spool, her eyes were lowered as she concentrated on its length.

"I got a kid too," she said.

"I know," he replied. His eyes, too, were on the reel.

"It's hard," she said.

Her apparent understanding lightened the fog around him. She was right, he thought. He knew nothing about raising a kid. And they said his son was picking over garbage.

It occurred to him that he had never heard one word from anyone about Katy's daughter. He bet that little girl did not grub around in the trash. Her mother would see to that. He looked with respect at the top of Katy's head.

"It is," he said.

A few minutes passed as she wound the line and placed it in a small brown paper bag. He handed her fifty cents and took a little longer than usual placing the coins in her small, brown hand.

He hesitated a few seconds more and then said.

"Um… could you ask your father if I could call on him this Friday evening? I have some business to talk over with him."

He knew and she knew that Matthew Stone never had any business to discuss these days. She did all the business. But Matthew Stone represented her system.

She looked up at John Finchley and knew she would do very well as mistress of his home, overseer of his lands and the power behind the mill and the yards. Marriage with him would be a nice step to a better life.

She tilted her head as if she were considering the suggestion.

"If you can wait a moment," she said. "I'll go and ask him."

Finchley leaned on the counter, abstractly studying the bean barrels, while she went out to the front porch where Matthew was making a slow but devastating move with his black checker. His opponent, Tom Foley, glowered unhappily.

Katy tapped her father on his shoulder. He started and almost knocked over the checkerboard.

"Wah!" he cried.

"Big John Finchley will be coming for dinner Friday," she said. "So don't get drunk before he gets there."

She turned on her heel and went back into the store. Her father shrugged and spat authoritatively into the spittoon. Foley made his final, but fatal move.

****

The sun shafted through mist over low tide and the sand was silver. Sandpipers scurried along the flat, shiny beach leaving rows of little crosses in their tread. Clams made mounds in the salt-coated surface as they burrowed deeper. Seagulls battled crows for positions on pilings.

Can and Little John sat silently, their backs against the bleached boards of the old boat. They were strange mirrors of each other; one much larger and grayer than the other but they were cut from the same cloth. They sat, legs splayed against the flat sand, their heads bent, counting their treasures. It had been a good haul.

Can was sorting the small nails, mostly bent and rusty, he had found behind the tavern. Little John had found several buttons and, under a fence, a big blue glass marble. Little John held it to the sun, marveling at the way the light gleamed through it, sending beams across the sand, his jeans and his bare feet.

Little John had learned a lot from Can. Things forgotten by people became precious once they were found.

Can had given him an old tin box for his treasures. The buttons and the marble would join several rusty hinges, part of a leather wallet and several pieces of broken china. When Little John went home, Can carefully placed the box in the sand under the prow of the boat for storage until the next morning.

Little John knew his things were safe close to Can's boat. Can was quiet and hairy and he smelled funny. But Can's eyes, glinting under bushy eyebrows, made Little John feel warm and calm.

Little John did not think of Can as Can and Can did not think of Little John as Little John. They had no need to attach labels to each other.

They sat counting pennies and looking at light through the marble until the sun slipped below the cotton clouds.

Little John knew it was almost time for him to go home.

A sudden shadow blocked the light between the sun and the boat and made the air cold.

Little John cried out as he looked up at his father's towering shape. The marble fell to the sand, where it would lie buried forever, never more to send the sun through its bright blue globe. Little John cried out again as his father's hand snaked out and jerked him into the air. Can also cried out as two more male figures ran around the boat and pulled the old man to his feet.

"Eh!" cried Garbage Can. "Eh!"

Was them come to get him? Garbage Can wondered.

Then he knew they finally had.

Little John screamed, shouted, wriggled and thrashed in his father's hard grasp. Tears poured down the boy's sandy face. His box of stuff tipped over and emptied out.

The deputy sheriffs took Can away but Little John was crying too hard to see him go.

****

Years later, Little John would come back to the beach but Can would not.

That day they took the old sailor to a clean, sand-free home where he was fed gravy paste and bread until he died one sunny summer morning, dreaming of the midget who walked with him in the tracks of a sandpiper while the crows and seagulls fought for space.

****

Little John would never know that. He only knew he was yelling and scratching at his father's hands when a fist landed on his ear and he felt pain in his head. Little John stopped squirming then but he kept sobbing as his bare feet scuffed the ground, making a wavy trail away from the beach, the pilings and the screeching gulls.

****

Five-year-old Sara squinted at the stitches she was setting in a tablecloth. The light from the kitchen window filtered through the rain, making it hard to see what she was doing. Milly would be mad. Sara sniffed and tried to blink away tears. She wanted to stop them but could not. They rose to her eyes and hurt her throat with a hollow hurt that would not go away.

She heard footsteps in the hallway and her mother's voice. She hoped her mother would not notice her, would not tell her how stupid she was. Sara knew that there were many, many things she must learn and that she would never be smart enough to learn them all, not ever.

Grandpa and a tall man who held a small boy by the wrist followed her mother into the room.

Sara was surprised and scared when they stood around her. She wished she could make herself very small, like an ant.

"My girl," announced Mother, pointing to her.

"Girl," repeated Grandpa, his nose hanging over her mother's shoulder.

"Ah. Girl," repeated the tall dark man, dragging the boy until he stood in front. The boy stared at Sara with very bright eyes and said nothing.

His legs seemed wobbly. Sara saw that the brightness in his eyes came from tears and the skin around his eyes was purple and puffy.

She knew what that was. The skin on her arms went like that when her mother grabbed her and hauled her up the stairs or down the stairs, or wherever she was being hauled to.

Sara knew the boy hurt so she lifted her eyes to his and tried to smile. His eyes were wary but deep in them Sara sensed a knowing that reached her.

It crept from his shiny brown eyes into her pale blue ones and it seemed for a moment as if the dark shadows around them faded

away. Sara understood that here was another like her, only this one
was a boy.

"My boy," announced the man. He bent over and looked into her
face.

"Your girl is good and clean," the man announced.

"She's good and clean," Mother agreed.

"Good?" Grandpa asked.

"Clean," Mother repeated firmly.

"My boy is called John," the man said. "The help call him Little
John."

"Mine is Sara. Say hello, Sara," Mother said.

"Hello," Sara said in a low voice.

"Shake hands, John," the man said

The boy held out a trembling bunch of fingers. Sara took them in
hers. They were rough and warm.

"Get up now and set the table!" Mother cried.

Sara put her sewing aside and walked over to the hutch. She
opened the drawers and took knives and forks, spoons and plates out
to the dining room.

The man dragged the boy outside and Sara heard the pump
running. She wondered why the boy wasn't taken to wash up in the
bathroom. The pump water was cold.

Sara and Little John ate their dinner at the kitchen table in silence
while the adults in the dining room talked about costs and board feet
and how lazy people were.

The big man, who Mother said she should call "Uncle John"
became a regular visitor.

Little John came with him every time. Mother told Uncle John
that all children must be kept busy with chores.

"Idle hands –" she said.

Uncle John agreed.

Little John hauled firewood, clipped bushes and dug the garden soil. Sara scrubbed floors, mended socks, weeded the garden and dusted furniture. They smiled shyly at each other when nobody was looking.

When they were both outside, Sara noticed that Little John stopped working every once in a while to stare at the sea.

When she saw him do that, she felt something in her go with him, go with him out to the silver dancing tide, out to the gray line of clouds on the horizon, out beyond the noise, the chores and the bruises that came their way when they did not do something right.

****

Summer was ending and gold streaked the dark green hills. Days were shorter and evening air sharp with wood smoke. Dogs barked at deer heading below the line of snow slipping lower to the valleys. Rifles echoed down gullies as elk shuddered and crashed to dead leaves. Red blood ran into the dirt as men gutted and skinned and argued about who got the hide and who got the meat.

Katy was making big plans. Big John had officially asked Matthew for permission to marry her. Matthew thought it was a wonderful idea because Big John was rich and owned good land.

Katy set conditions for the union. Business was business. After the wedding, she would hire someone to work in the store. After she moved into Big John's big house on the hill, she would refurnish it and redecorate it. She required a housekeeper and a cook.

The children would be starting school in the fall. As Mrs. John Finchley, the schoolhouse in Abraham was not good enough for her Katy.

It could certainly not provide Little John with enough discipline. She thought the two would be better off in boarding schools.

"Then I can concentrate on running your house," Katy told Big John. "Meanwhile, your boy needs someone to watch him until after the wedding. Milly already watches Sara"

Big John liked the plan. The children were family. They were to be Finchleys. They needed to learn how to be around people with money and education and discipline. Anyway, his son made him feel uneasy and he never had understood girl children. He hired Rob, who had hurt his back at the mill, as Little John's watchdog and instructed him to keep the boy very busy, away from the beach and away from Aunt Audrey.

"That woman is too flighty," Katy sniffed.

Little John withdrew into himself. He was just waiting now, waiting to be moved on. His little-boy soul curled up behind his round, dark eyes and went to sleep. It was waiting for a kiss or a hug to wake it up.

But his soul would sleep for a long time because there were no magic kisses or hugs for Little John, no safe place for him to go. He felt scared and cold. In his dreams, he was lost in a dark forest where elk blood soaked dying leaves and vines crawled.

****

Big John was surprised to see how involved Katy was in the wedding ceremony and the elaborate reception. He thought her taste would be simpler. But Katy saw this opportunity to be better, bigger than any other Stone, to carry more weight around town.

She was rich now and everybody should know it.

On the day, the Methodist Church was filled to overflowing with people who knew that their job, their credit at the hardware store – in fact their whole standing in town – depended on their attendance at Big John Finchley's wedding.

Little John and Sara walked behind the couple like two wind-up dolls, Little John in brown velvet and Sara in blue. The adults at the ceremony, who took the time to look into Little John's eyes, looked away uneasily, felt guilty for a second and then forgot. They did not look at him again.

Sara's eyelids were lowered. She looked pretty so nobody bothered to look further. She was only a girl. Nobody looked into her eyes. They looked at her hair and her dress so Sara was safe from attack because nobody knew she was there.

The faces in the pews wore smiles that remained carefully in place at the reception afterwards in the big house, catered by a Portland company with uniformed maids.

No pickled kelp was on the rented round tables covered by bright white linen. Instead, the guests picked nervously at miniscule arrangements of meat, cheese and seafood. There just was enough champagne to provide each guest with one glass for the marital toast.

Fortunately, Slick, Mitch, Beaner and their friends had brought along flasks of whisky hidden in their jackets. They survived the required time at the reception before going to the tavern and a more raucous, much more energetic, gathering.

"Those kids are strange," Slick said over his beer.

"They sure are," everybody agreed. The conversation shifted to a discussion of the unfulfilling food at the reception.

****

Little John stared at a small suitcase on the chair beside his bed and the stiff new clothes folded on top of it.

"That's your'n," Rob said, pointing to the suitcase. "You're taking it off to school with you."

Little John waited impassively by the bed. Rob looked down at him and frowned.

"They're sendin' you off to a tough school," Rob said harshly. "It's military. You'll shape up there. They'll be real rough on you. We're leaving first thing in the morning."

Rob wished the kid would react in some way remotely childlike, remotely normal. Little John stood still, waiting to find out where and how he was to move next.

He did not feel any curiosity or anger or sadness. He just knew he needed to wait and see.

Rob looked at the expressionless child and left.

"Weird," he muttered.

Little John put himself to bed. By dawn, he was dressed and was ready for Rob. The house was silent when they left for the station. Nobody came to say goodbye.

As they walked to the car, Little John looked up at the big house. There was a light on in an upstairs room. Sara stood by the window looking down at the drive. Her hair gleamed like a halo in the light behind her. Something inside him flickered.

After a few days on the train, Rob took him to a large brick place where there were many other boys with blank eyes and scared faces.

They were controlled by larger men in dark clothes and big boots who told everybody what to do and when to do it. So Little John kept on moving where and how he was told, while his soul slept on.

****

Milly took Sara to her school in California the next day. Grassy slopes and small, cultivated trees surrounded the ocean-side campus.

Sara liked it there. It was a much easier life than she had known. She liked sewing, sitting on the grass during the picnics and making clay animals during art class. She found it easy to follow the rules, and while she never revealed enough of herself to make close friends, she was generally accepted by the other girls.

She was happiest when she was in the school's library. There, she could escape to new worlds where nobody could reach her. She populated her mind with the wonderful new friends she met in the pages of novels. She dreamed about *The Secret Garden*, helped Nancy Drew solve mysteries and shared John Brown's school days. Her mind was nourished by the diet of places and people far from the room where she strained her eyes on the printed words in poems and books. Years later, she remembered every detail about the characters in the novels she read but she never could recall the names of her classmates or the faces of her teachers.

For Sara and Little John, the school terms passed with predictable routine. Summers at their respective summer camps came and went as uneventfully. At camp, Sara read outdoors under stunted trees in the California hills and Little John marched outdoors through the Minnesota woods.

They both went back to Abraham for the Christmas holidays, where Katy made sure they were kept busy with chores. On Christmas mornings, Little John and Sara sat on the sofa near the tree to open the presents selected for them by the housekeeper. They remained on the sofa without speaking as Katy and Big John hosted the annual gathering of business contacts who had been invited to the Finchley mansion.

Chapter Three

The fireplace chimney caught fire on Christmas morning the year that Little John turned thirteen and Sara, twelve. Black sooty smoke filled the living room. Little John, Sara, Katy, Big John, the guests and the servants ran outside.

Sara and Little John, realizing that nobody was noticing them, kept on running – out of the yard, down the path and down to the beach. It was raining so they found shelter under a drift log. It had once been a cedar stump, and now, tipped over and bleached white, it provided a safe haven in its gnarled roots.

They huddled together on the dry white sand. They watched the rain sleet sideways against the white foaming waves that crashed and spread over pebbles and sand. They heard drums in the beating surf.

Little John put his arms around Sara to keep her warm and, then, on a sudden impulse, kissed her hair. She lay back in his arms. They remained in that position until dusk, when the last of the fire engines drove away from the house. They walked home holding hands but entered the front door separately. Nobody had missed them.

From then on, during each winter break, they found ways to sneak away from the house to the warmth of their driftwood cave. Sara talked about the books she read. Little John talked about the music he heard in his head.

Two more winters passed. That Christmas, Katy entertained an exceptionally demanding couple of guests. They wanted drink after drink and would not stop talking about their real estate deals. Katy had to listen.

In any case, Katy's "real" son Philip, born three years after the wedding, had replaced Sara and Little John as the object of her attention. It was much easier for Little John and Sara to escape unnoticed and arrive at the beach as dusk fell.

"No rain," Sara said happily, as they settled into their driftwood cave.

Wisps of foam floated on low tide ripples.

"It's warm for this time of year," Little John said.

He looked down at her. The setting sun stained her blond hair pink. Her skin was like the petals of a white rose. He shifted uncomfortably.

"So what's the new book this year?" he asked, trying to ignore the pressure forming in his groin.

"A girl in my dorm snuck in *Lady Chatterley's Lover*," Sara said. Her eyes seemed to get darker as she spoke.

"What's that?"

"It was written in 1928 by D.H. Lawrence and was banned in this country for years. We read it out loud by candlelight. Wow."

"Banned? Why?"

"Too sexy. It was very sexy. But beautiful."

"A guy in my dorm smuggled in copies of *Playboy* magazine," he said. "Now *that* was sexy. Those women were completely naked."

"*Lady Chatterley's Lover* is great literature as well as being sexy," she told him, sounding, he thought, like his English teacher, sort of snooty.

"What's so great about it?" he asked huffily.

"Lawrence makes the point that we should be free to express ourselves sexually and that we lose freedoms when we obey the conventions imposed by class or by money," she explained carefully, and even more snootily, he thought.

"Yeah. OK," he drawled.

"Oh well, he's *right*!" she asserted.

"Playboy is literature, too," he said. His voice tailed off has he remembered the sweet bulging breasts of the centerfolds. This is getting really tough, he thought. Part of him hurt.

He looked down at her again. Her expression was strange. Her white eyebrows had a slight furrow between them.

She reached up and stroked his face.

His breath caught and he slowly leaned towards her until their lips met.

Hers were velvet. His hands stroked her budding nipples until they hardened beneath his touch.

She felt his hand and a new, powerful feeling went from her lips to her thighs. She felt herself wanting, wanting....

Is this how it feels? she wondered.

His hand went under her skirt and touched the cotton of her panties. She lay back on the sand and helped him pull them off. They took off his trousers and shirt and her blouse and skirt until they were naked, their discarded clothes between them and the cold sand.

She spread her legs as he rose over her. He did not enter her right away, although he wanted to very much but he had read and thought about it and did not want to hurt her. He wanted her to be ready, ready for him, so he held back and kissed her even as he swelled and hurt.

But then her hips were thrusting against his and she was open and moist so together they became as a laughing lotus, curled petals of a single form, moving as one, sounding notes of joy. Then the universe opened for them so, for a while, they lay curled into each other in their driftwood cave as the sun slipped, bleeding, into the pale white sea.

****

Katy did not notice them when they came back. Philip was screaming. Philip was a large-sized, angry child who frequently bellowed his displeasure at the top of his lungs. Katy and the nurse were trying to settle him down as Sara and Little John walked quietly through the living room and upstairs to their rooms.

Sara stared at her image in her mirror. As far as she could see, she looked the same. She took off her stained panties, washed them in the sink, changed out of her sandy clothes and went to bed.

Little John lay awake for several hours. The sound of the surf, her smell, her touch and their ecstasy formed a new rhythm and his first song was born.

****

Philip screamed all night, every night.

"Strong boy, strong lungs," Katy uttered as she handed the wriggling noisemaker back to the expensive nursemaid she had shipped in from Los Angeles. Katy knew Philip would go far because his bloodlines were better, stronger and more predictable. He was determined and he was strong, even if he was noisy.

Katy focused on her role as the leading lady of Abraham by traveling out of town to buy linens, carpets, art, furniture and exotic plants.

New furniture moved in and out of the mansion as quickly as did her servants. Katy needed to stay "in style" so she regularly had the old pieces delivered to a second-hand store in Portland where they sold for a healthy commission. She went to San Francisco to find fashionable replacements.

At first, she thought Boston would be the best place to set standards for taste in Abraham. So she went to Boston to buy a sideboard and came back empty-handed.

"They got no taste. Them Easterners are too pushy," Katy said.

She had failed to buy the sideboard because it sold to a Bostonite who knew the store's owner. The owner had never heard of Finchley Incorporated.

"Too pushy by far," Katy repeated.

Big John agreed. Everybody should have heard of Finchley Incorporated by now.

Under Katy's guidance, he had worked hard to make sure the name, Finchley Incorporated, was known across the country. He hired executives and public relations practitioners. As more people took on the day-to-day operations of his businesses, he played golf with competitors and associates and traveled to all-male conventions and retreats.

He let Katy take over responsibilities for the children, particularly Philip. Philip annoyed him. He could not feel any affection for the child.

I guess I just don't like kids, he told himself.

When Big John allowed himself to think about it, he remembered the quiet nature of his oldest son, remembered their dinners together when Little John had been very young and thought he should write the boy at school. He never got around to it. So many other things got in the way.

He also remembered John's mother and the feeling he had when he was with her. At the time he hadn't noticed it but he didn't have it now.

Katy no longer appealed to him physically. He looked inside himself but could not find any emotion associated with her beyond the respect he had for anybody who worked for him and did their jobs well.

He tried to stop thinking about Katy or Philip, although he derived a great deal of satisfaction from his public image as a family man. His bloodline had been extended by not one but two sons.

He felt proud when he realized that his sons and his sons' sons could have an important and wealthy heritage. They would never have to stumble over beach rocks in search of a new beginning.

However, once in a while, as he stood at the window of his bedroom and watched the sun set over the churning sea, Big John was hypnotized by the flat and hazy line where the sky and sea melted together. During that time, he felt unfinished, as if something were slipping away from him. He was glad when the feeling faded as the sea swallowed the light, allowing him to go back to business.

After a couple of years, Katy noticed that her husband avoided Philip. Big John left the room when the child was present.

"Philip will be running things once the old man's gone and Philip will own it all, if I have anything to say about it. Philip is interested in the family business, not like John Jr. He's just different. Who knows, he may not really be a Finchley, anyhow. That Janice could have been with anybody; she was that strange," Katy told Milly, who was the only domestic she had not fired after less than six months of service.

"I'm used to her," Milly told them at the tavern. "I'm the only one who knows what's what. The new ones have to come to me for advice."

To keep Philip underfoot and obvious, Katy hired tutors to homeschool the boy. Philip threw tantrums and items at his teachers. They quit quickly. Katy replaced them just as quickly.

"He's high strung," she told the new candidates.

"He's impossible," they told her as they left.

As Finchley Incorporated grew, so did the town of Abraham. Big John sold some of his land north of town to a developer who cleared it and built the Abraham Country Club. Big John and Katy were founding members.

Katy teased her hair into a pale blonde beehive and bought lime-green pedal pushers. Big John learned to play golf. Philip learned to eat Twinkies.

By the end of the fabulous fifties, Big John was almost retired. When he was not playing golf or going to conventions, he sat on a maroon, nubby couch in the living room and watched the world bop by on a round television screen, eating dinner from a TV tray.

Philip continued to expand his waistline. As his girth broadened, his mind shrank as if he had to make room for all the extra fat around his ears. As his tutors came and went, the only information he absorbed had to do with himself, his entitlement to the family money and all the things he would do once he had it all.

There was a world out there he was not allowed to share. He hated his life in the big house and wanted to be like the kids on television and in the movies he saw at the Abraham Theatre every Saturday. He wanted to be a Mouseketeer. He wanted to meet Tammie and surf. His stepbrother and sister had lives. They got to leave.

The portion of his brain fed by envy and anger remained well nourished. In this way, Philip stumbled through puberty, under disciplined, under socialized and overfed. Any thought of his stepbrother John and his sister, Sara, sent him straight to the refrigerator where he swallowed anything he found inside it.

Chapter Four

By the time Little John was in his senior year, he knew he hated military discipline and would never make it part of his life once he got out of school.

While the war in Vietnam inspired some of the others in his class with dreams of glory, Little John and his friends shared underground newspapers and talked about how to hide from the system.

After dark in the dorm, they whispered about how they could avoid the draft and never be considered good enough for any service selecting only the healthiest young men to be blown apart, maimed, rendered insane and incapable of feeling guilt.

As he stood at attention during the graduation ceremony, Little John listened to a colonel who was delivering the commencement address and planned his escape.

He knew that no Finchley was in the audience. Big John had sent a note containing congratulations, an apology for his absence at the ceremony due to an important business meeting and a one-hundred dollar bill. Katy did not bother to send an excuse and did not attend. Sara was still trapped at her school for another year.

After the caps were tossed and the other cadets mingled with family, Little John went back to his room, put the uniform on the bed, pulled on civilian jeans and T-shirt, put the bill and a few dollars left from his allowance into his pocket and left the academy grounds.

He hitchhiked to Portland where he found an anti-war commune his friends had told him about.

There, he tumbled into a lava-lamp world of pot and pills, LSD and music. He found a 12-string guitar in a pawnshop and he learned how to play it. His inspiration came from Mississippi John Hurt and the sitar music of Ravi Shankar, at the time impacting musicians from the California beaches to British boy bands.

He remembered the music that roared in his ears with the winter storms, the driving rain and the wind. Now it echoed from his guitar. As he played and sang, he heard the rhythm of the pounding waves from the shores below Abraham. He thought of Aunt Audrey and Uncle Gary as he sang "Make Me A Pallet on Your Floor."

Unfortunately, although women in the commune prepared plates of brown rice and bowls of soup, Little John often forget to eat as he swallowed pills, smoked pot and strummed through acid-inspired dreams and trips.

One morning, he could not stop throwing up.

"Man, you got to get help," the girl beside him on the mattress said. "You are making the place stink."

He nodded and drank the bottle of Pepto-Bismol she handed him. "I got an aunt up the coast," he mumbled.

"Groovy," the girl said. "I'll drive you there."

A few days later, Audrey looked up from the pile of newly polished agates she was sorting to see a multi-colored VW van pull up in front of the house.

Little John stumbled out of it, a pack on his back and a guitar case in his hand. His hair had grown long and greasy. His clothes were rags and he was pale as sea foam.

Audrey barely recognized him.

"I'm sick," he said as she approached.

"Why, you poor thing! Come on in. Gary will be so glad to see you!"

Once Little John was settled on the couch sipping a bowl of chicken soup, he noticed that Uncle Gary was huddled in the easy chair across the room, wrapped in a blanket. Uncle Gary seemed to have shrunk.

"What's the matter?" Little John asked, forgetting his own problems. "What's wrong?"

Uncle Gary's eyes were hollow but filled with gentleness. "It is the cancer," he said. "It's got me."

Little John was sad when he found out that Gary was too sick to play guitar. Instead, he listened to recordings of John Philip Sousa's marches.

As Little John grew better, he began to play them as Uncle Gary smiled and Aunt Audrey sighed.

Soon, Little John could replicate the sound of every instrument in the bands. As he played, the drums beat, the horns wailed and cymbals crashed.

Little John and his uncle whispered the words of "The Teddy Bears Picnic" as Little John added harmonics to the melody.

"For ev'ry bear that ever there was will gather there for certain, because... today's the day the Teddy Bears have their picnic."

In a couple of months, Little John had cleaned out his system and was inhaling the sea wind as he walked along the beach. He tried to find Can but the old boat had long been washed away. He heard the grating roar of pebbles as the tide changed.

Lines from a poem that Sara used to read him came to his mind.

...and fling, at their return, up the high strand, began and cease, and then again begin with tremulous cadence slow, and so bring the eternal note of sadness in.

He played guitar as he sat against a beached log, sending his tunes over the Pacific Ocean. He hoped they would float across to fight the far off noises in the jungles, *where ignorant armies clashed by night.*

During those weeks, Little John did not see Big John or Katy. His father was doing business in Florida and Little John had no desire to visit Katy or Philip. He did write to Sara explaining that he had found music and his soul and was traveling to new places in his head. He signed the letter "Barefoot John," the name he used as a performer.

After a while, he felt he was imposing on his aunt and knew the couple needed to spend their last weeks alone with each other before Gary's soul drifted out to sea.

Aunt Audrey was not surprised when Little John said he was going to Seattle because he had never been there before and he wanted to check that scene out.

"I'll miss you. Stay in touch," she said.

The next day, she drove him to the Abraham bus station. He had originally intended to hitchhike but she talked him put of it by pointing out how little traffic actually came through Abraham and by buying him a bus ticket.

At the Seattle bus depot, he met another musician who introduced him to the underworld around Puget Sound.

He soon was stoned again. He lost himself on the cobbled streets that wound up from the waterfront. He slept in the back rooms of the coffee houses where pot and patchouli mingled in an acrid mist.

After several weeks, Audrey wondered why he did not call her but Gary was now very ill and demanded most of her attention. She tried not to think too much about her nephew.

****

One day, while Little John was browsing through a pawnshop, he found a monocle that he placed over his right eye.

He thought it added to his image. His new friends were proud of the fact that while they had once been known only as "fringies," because of their existence on the fringes of society – now they were called "hippies" and associated with the hip world of jazz and dream-filled pot pipes.

High as the clouds, Little John wandered the streets of old Seattle and up Capitol Hill looking for "groovies" in garbage cans. At Pike

Market, he collected donations in his open guitar case as he played Sousa marches and Hurt blues.

Another six months drifted by. Little John was unaware of the passing of time or even what day of the week it was. He never had an address so letters from the draft board went to Big John in Abraham.

Big John ignored them. He had an idea that he did not want to know what his oldest son was doing and avoided the issue by refusing to think about it.

Then Little John came to earth long enough to think about Aunt Audrey and Uncle Gary and placed a collect call. He was so bombed as he spoke, so scrambled that she decided she had to talk to Big John about him.

Gary told her not her to meddle.

"That old bastard doesn't give a shit about the kid," he said.

Audrey's lips tightened; a rare expression of frustration came over her usually placid face. She hated to go against Gary's wishes.

"Maybe," she replied. "But Little John is his first-born. That man has got to do something about the boy. Send him money. Help him out."

She scurried through her agate-lined yard, out the white swinging gate, down the gully and up the asphalt driveway to her brother-in-law's house.

Audrey walked in on Big John, Katy and Philip in the living room.

"Your son is living out of garbage cans again," she announced.

Big John looked up. "What do you mean?"

He glanced across the room at Philip, who pursed his lips and nodded with "I'm not surprised" written all over his pudgy face. Big John grimaced.

Philip's home schooling had given the boy a high level of arrogance. Years of intimidating tutors made him certain of his power and although he was too young to be drafted, he often told his father that he wished that he was old enough to go off to fight for America in Vietnam.

Big John remembered the humiliation that drove him into marriage with Katy.

"Damn," Big John said, thinking of the letters from the draft board on his desk. "Where is he? I better let that draft board know. Perhaps being in the service will knock some sense into him."

Audrey looked at her brother-in-law in disgust. That man did not have a shred of understanding for his oldest son. How would sending Little John off to war help?

But something needed to be done. Perhaps college. Then he wouldn't get drafted.

"I think he'd do better in school," she said.

Big John grunted.

"He's still got to go to the draft board. You know how to reach him?"

Audrey paused before she answered. Was this the right thing to do?

"I just have the number of the coffee house in Seattle he called me from. It's near the University of Washington. Perhaps they can get a message to him," she said.

She gave Big John the number and walked home with a heavy step.

****

Gary asked "That man gonna do anything?"

"I don't know," Audrey replied.

"Told you," Gary muttered with more triumph in his tone than he felt. He hated to see Audrey worried. She was such a good woman and he loved her so very much. Audrey decided to write to Sara at

school and tell her about Little John's problems. Sara was due to
graduate and would be coming home. Maybe she could do
something.

****

Little John was coming down from an acid trip when he
wandered into the Aggervawn coffee house in Seattle's University
District. The owner, Moon Rose, told him the draft board had called
her. They were looking for him.

"Man," she said. Her hands fluttered over her tie-dyed skirt like
birds. "They said they was comin' here to get you if you don't show
up there tomorrow morning. You can't let them do that. It would be
a major bummer if they came here."

Little John peered at her through his non-monocled eye.
"Riiiiiight," he drawled. "You better get me some stuff."

****

When Little John showed up at the draft board office the next
morning, he was as stoned as he could get and full of substances that
rendered his urine unfit for army issue. He was dehydrated, had a
rapid heart beat and couldn't blow hard enough to move a feather.
His eyes were bloodshot and his hands shook. He told Moon Rose
later that he really "freaked out the doc."

****

The letter from the Seattle University District draft board arrived
at Abraham a week later. It indicated Little John had been judged
unfit for military service. Big John was furious.

He lost his usual calm as he cursed and decided that his oldest
son had not only dishonored him but had also dishonored his
country. Finchley men were supposed to be leaders not weaklings. It

made no sense. Little John had done pretty well at sports at the academy. What had gone wrong?

The next day Big John drove to Seattle. He marched into a dusty room where a depressed-looking duty officer hunched over stacks of papers on a too-small desk. Big John did not realize that this particular duty officer was happy to reject young men from service, whenever that rejection was according to the rules. The duty officer did not like the fact that so many of the young faces he saw across from him would never be seen again. Also, he had never been able to understand why this particular war was raging, in any case.

The duty officer took an instant dislike to Big John's blustering patriotism. He enjoyed telling the sputtering old man that his son had giggled, told the doctor he was also known as Little Peter and waved his penis at the examining physician. The officer added that the young man said that the finger felt good when inserted in his rectum and asked the doctor to do it again. In conclusion, the duty officer told Big John that his son, John, was probably insane, was certainly on drugs and possibly homosexual.

Breaking the speed limit along most of Highway 99, Big John drove straight from Seattle to Portland to visit Rolled, Smythe and Right. Something had to be done. Something had to be set up to protect his son, even if all those things were true. But they couldn't be. Could they? Perhaps Janice had given her son her strangeness, her way of being different.

Was the boy that different? Perhaps he could be forced into school, forced into growing up.

In his office in downtown Portland, lawyer George Right suggested that Big John establish a trust fund in Little John's name. It would be designed so that Little John would not control the trust funds until he turned thirty-five.

"Or until he convinces you he is reliable enough for you to change the terms," Right added.

Until then Right said the trust would pay Little John's tuition at college as well as any bills for food, clothing or shelter – within reason.

Big John considered the matter.

"How can you get him into the school?"

"His grades were good enough at the academy. We can apply for his admission to the University of Washington in Seattle, where he is apparently now living. Once he has been accepted, we will send one of our people up there to make sure he registers for classes."

Big John nodded. "Why thirty-five?" he asked.

"It's a standard age we use in situations like this. If he can't get control of his trust funds until he is thirty-five years old, he may be motivated to improve himself. He's only nineteen now. At the same time, we make sure he doesn't starve."

After Big John left the office, Right rolled back his brown leather chair and gazed through the tinted glass of his floor-to-ceiling window at Portland's Main Street below. A group of Hare Krishnas drummed and collected donations on the corner. From his vantage point they looked like large yellow flowers with pink centers punctuated by ponytails.

Right wondered what Big John Finchley's kid looked like. Finchley's attitude made him feel some sympathy for the young man. Right turned back to his desk and pressed a button on the intercom.

"Send in Shirley," he said.

Shirley McBride would be ideal for the job, he thought. She had just joined the firm, was not a partner and had yet to prove herself. The kid probably needed the maternal touch.

****

Shirley was at first offended and then intrigued by her new assignment. She knew that few women went through law school and even fewer actually found work in a law firm. She remembered how, during her high school days in Eugene, she had been called Beluga Shirley and knew that she was too fat to find a husband. This had motivated her to study hard and sail through law school and the bar exams without skipping a beat.

Her father, who owned a chain or hardware stores, had been happy to invest in her education. Otherwise, they both knew, he'd be supporting her for the rest of her life and he had better things to do with his money.

Shirley kept her dark hair short, hid her brilliant eyes behind thick glasses and wore large, black flowing garments. Her father bought her a blue Super VW beetle she called Griselda. She loved the way she filled the car with her person.

"Griselda feels like my skin," she told her friends. "It's all me on the road. Not just a human rattling around in an alien container."

Although Shirley had little patience with hippies and draft dodgers, her assignment to track down and help a young man gone astray interested her.

She decided it would be a nice challenge to get the boy started in college. So, after she obtained Little John's transcripts, she used her power-of-attorney and applied for his entry to classes at the University of Washington. He was accepted.

By then, it was mid-September and classes started in three weeks. Little John had to register in person.

The problem was, nobody knew where he was. He had no known address. She called John Finchley in Abraham. He had no idea where his son was and sounded irritated when she asked him for a contact point. He suggested she call the boy's aunt, Audrey Smith. Audrey told her that Little John liked to play guitar at the Aggervawn coffee house in Seattle's University District.

The woman's voice on the end of the telephone at the coffee house was vague and uncommunicative. Those hippies do stick together, Shirley mused. She decided to check out the place in person.

A weekend in Seattle will be fun, she thought as she drove Griselda up Highway 99.

The sun brightened a clear blue sky. The brilliant reds and purples of sumac and vine maple dappled the rolling hills on either side of the Columbia River. Tall firs crowded the edges of the two-lane highway until they gave way to dairy farms and acres of apple trees, strawberry fields and sharp-edged white houses protected from the wind by stands of blowing poplars.

A little south of Fort Lewis, Shirley found herself stuck behind a line of army tanks, trucks and staff cars. She wondered if there would ever be four-lane highway all the way to Seattle. She doubted it; there were not enough people.

The highway wound along the waterfront, passed the Smith Tower, crossed the Fremont Bridge and up to the University District. Shirley took a left on 48th Street and began looking for a motel.

She found a room in a newly built Motel 6 and happily paid the ten dollars for the night. She knew there were cheaper places but this was clean and close to her search area.

After splashing some water on her face, she unpacked her bag and left her room. She asked the clerk in the office if he had ever heard of the Aggervawn coffee house. He nodded and frowned.

"Where is it precisely?" she asked.

"It's up on University Avenue, Ma'am. But you won't want to go there."

"Why not?"

He was a sharp-faced little man, with clumps of hair ringing a gleaming red scalp. His small brown eyes shifted sideways as he tilted his head to look at her speculatively.

"It's full of them commies and hippies. You wouldn't like it."

Shirley stared down at him and asked calmly.

"What's the address, please?"

He shrugged, gave her the street number and told her it was opposite Black Star Pawn.

The Aggervawn was easy to find. So was Little John.

Once she pushed aside the strings of silver beads across the entrance to the smoke-filled, candlelit room, she saw a young man who matched his description balanced on the edge of a wooden kitchen chair. It was tilted precariously against the burlap-covered wall. His head leaned back as he strummed the guitar lying across his lap and his bare feet dangled. His monocle caught the flames of the candles that flickered on worn tables. His shoulder-length dark curls trembled in the rolling rhythm.

There were other people in the room. They were decorated with beads, feathers, tie-dyed fabrics and crystals. The men wore blue work shirts embroidered with mandalas. The women were like brightly colored birds. Everyone was smiling.

They're all stoned, Shirley thought.

Shirley found a seat in a corner and listened to the music. A tall, unusually thin woman offered her some gingerbread.

A small, pale young man sold her a cup of espresso. Shirley watched Little John's fingers dance on the strings.

Years later, she would still recall the clarity of his notes. They would be in her ears, she knew, until her hearing died.

One set slow bell would seem to toll,
the remembrance of the sweetest soul,
that ever looked with human eyes.

Little John sang the blues with hypnotic power. Shirley suddenly was a little afraid of him and of where she was.

Then he was done. A woman with a dulcimer filled the room with plaintiff song and harmonic chords. Shirley gestured to the gingerbread saleswoman.

"Can you give a message to John over there?" Shirley whispered.

The woman hesitated.

"He is John Finchley, isn't he?" Shirley persisted.

"It's Barefoot John," the woman muttered, her face hardening with suspicion.

"What do you want?"

Shirley tried to smile reassuringly. She groped for the right words to identify herself.

"I'm his lawyer," she said finally. "Tell him I'm from his father, John Finchley, senior."

The woman looked puzzled but after giving Shirley another wary glance, moved over to Little John and whispered to him.

The monocle swung in Shirley's direction. Little John propped his guitar against the wall and stood up. He walked across the room, stood in front of her and jerked his head to one side. She understood he wanted her to go with him so their conversation would not disturb the music.

Shirley followed Little John out to a small brick courtyard behind the building. She noticed that he was much shorter than she was and that his feet were bare and filthy. The shoulders emerging from the ragged edges of his sleeveless T-shirt were muscular and well formed.

Little John leaned against the wall and waited for her to speak.

"Your father has arranged for you to take classes at the University of Washington," she said, deciding to get straight to the point. "He'll also provide you with food, shelter and clothing."

"Groovy," Little John commented and fell silent.

Shirley looked at him, startled. He did not seem to be surprised. He studied her with his one visible eye. She waited. He said nothing.

"Don't you want to know how this will work?" she asked.

"Sure," he replied amiably.

"Well," she said, pressing on, feeling as if she were pushing her way through a swamp. "Tomorrow I can take you to register for your classes."

"Cool," he agreed.

She blinked and forged ahead. "Where can I meet you?"

Now he looked puzzled. A slight frown formed between his eyebrows, as if predicting his whereabouts was an unfamiliar process.

"Here?" he asked, as if she should know.

"Can you be here by ten tomorrow morning?"

"Sure."

He turned away from her, wandered back inside and disappeared into the smoke. He had obviously finished communicating. Shirley waited for a few seconds, sighed, walked back to her car and went to her motel.

After a restless night, she rose, showered, ate a large breakfast at Little Black Sambo's Pancake House across the street and went back to the Aggervawn. It was a bright and sunny morning but the interior of the coffee house was as dark as it had been the evening before.

She was surprised to find it open although there were no customers. Nobody came out of the kitchen when she stepped inside.

Then she saw Little John, rocking back on the same chair as the night before, playing guitar and swinging his bare feet.

"Great!" she cried, because she had been prepared for him not to be there and had wondered what to do if that happened.

He said nothing but kept on strumming his guitar.

She sat beside him, feeling that this morning she could be a little more familiar. She noticed he was wearing the same clothes he had on the night before. It occurred to her that he should clean up a little before he registered for his classes.

"Do you need to change?" she asked him.

He shook his head.

"Er, what about shoes?" she asked.

He sighed heavily and looked at her as if she had demanded to see him naked. "I'll get them," he said.

He stood up and carried his guitar back into the kitchen. Shirley heard some voices.

He came back into the room without his guitar but wearing clogs with wooden soles. As he approached her, a blast of sweet, pine-scented air followed.

Pot for breakfast, Shirley mused.

Little John's personal odor was also noticeable.

"Do you need to shower before we go through registration?" she asked.

"Showering washes away your natural juices," he informed her.

Shirley realized she would have to tolerate Little John's body scent and hoped they would not spend too much time in confined quarters. She stood up.

"Well then, let's go," she said.

Little John's naturalness was very evident inside Griselda so Shirley drove with the windows open. He remained silent as he walked up the steps behind her into the University of Washington admissions building. He waited patiently for his turn in front of the registration desk and was unperturbed by the confusion caused by the fact that his fees had been paid although he was not yet registered.

Shirley was less patient but she explained, explained and explained again. Little John stayed awake long enough to sign the cards for three courses.

Little John said vaguely he stayed "with friends" when the registrar wanted his address. Shirley's business address and telephone number were recorded instead. Shirley promised the frustrated registrar she would update Little John's address as soon as she could.

During the final stages of his registration, he curled up in a chair and dozed off. Shirley finished the process for him and then woke him up.

At two o'clock that afternoon, Shirley drove Little John back to the Aggervawn.

"Now we need to find you a place to live. I'll start looking tomorrow. Do you want to come with me?"

He shook his head.

"I'll find something for you tomorrow morning and I'll be back here at about four o'clock tomorrow afternoon to let you know where it is."

"Groovy," said Little John and drifted back into the kitchen.

Shirley found him a one-bedroom apartment opposite the main entrance to the university. The manager at first was suspicious and reluctant to rent to an unseen tenant. She gave him her business card told him to call her if there were any problems.

She said she would pay six months' rent and any other fees for utilities in advance and would continue to pay him regularly after that. He relaxed, accepted her check and gave her the key.

When Shirley, flushed with victory, arrived at the Aggervawn, Little John was not there, neither were his guitar or his earth shoes. Moon Rose, the gingerbread saleswoman, told Shirley that Little John had "split."

Her small pale husband, Zack, added that Little John probably had a "gig" but he didn't know where.

Shirley felt defeated but still determined.

She stayed in Seattle two more days but there was no sign of Little John. By then she had spent so much time at the Aggervawn she was accepted, and, because she bought large quantities of gingerbread and tipped lavishly, was appreciated. She made friends with Moon Rose and Zack.

On Tuesday, Shirley gave Little John's apartment key with an explanatory note to Moon Rose who promised to explain the arrangements to Little John, as soon as he came by again. Shirley drove Griselda back to Portland.

Little John did get the message a week later but never showed up at the apartment. Moon Rose called Shirley and told her that he tried to find the building but got lost. He returned to the coffee house and gave Moon Rose back the key, saying he'd try again someday. Moon Rose said Little John had also tried to find his classes at the University but got lost then too.

Moon Rose did not need to tell Shirley that so many drugs fogged Little John's mind – so much acid sent colored streamers across his eyes – that finding anything had become impossible for him. He floated away from time, reality and any obligations. Only his music still tolled through the night.

After several more weeks passed, Moon Rose telephoned Shirley and told her that Little John was flying more loosely tethered than usual and hardly ever landed. He sometimes did not eat for a day or two because he forgot about food, although he never stopped playing his guitar.

"It's kind of like a magic carpet," Moon Rose mused. "He floats on the notes."

"He still needs to eat," Shirley muttered crossly.

Moon Rose's cousins, Jan and Eva Zbeicki, owned the Café Korner, a block up the street from the Aggervawn. It served wholesome food and catered to students and artistic types who preferred brown to white rice and wanted alfalfa sprouts on everything.

"He stops in there from time to time," Moon Rose told Shirley.

Shirley sighed and called up the Zbeickis. She arranged to send them a check every month, providing they sent her receipts indicating that Little John ate there at least once a day.

The plan seemed to work, although Shirley decided Little John must be gaining a great deal of weight, considering the size of the monthly bill she received.

****

Little John liked the cooking at the Café Korner and the fact that he could wander in at any time of the day or night and stay as long as he wanted. They let him sleep in a chair when he felt like it and they never stopped his music. His playing drew people to him and into the Café. Jan and Eva made a healthy profit since anything John's friends ate was billed to Rolled, Smythe and Right.

Little John's friends like the free food almost as much as they liked his music so he was soon surrounded by a devoted audience.

On his stool in the Café, Little John composed new songs and taught them to the would-be musicians who strummed along with him.

His soul winged into the sun on the strings of his guitar. He was moving, still moving on, but now he was blown around by music, like a bright leaf twirling in the autumn wind.

Little John lived on the fringes of his world, sometimes sleeping in the park, sometimes in the Café and sometimes with red-haired hippie girls who satisfied him physically. They loved him, laughed when they were stoned and came to the Café or the Aggervawn to hear him play.

"Koozie!" he called them, "Koozie!"

Once, he spent the night in the King County jail. He had been arrested while playing guitar for a group of anti-war protesters sitting outside the Federal Building. Moon Rose called Shirley who drove to Seattle and paid his bail. Moon Rose and Shirley kept Little John in their sight until his trial the following Monday, where Shirley made sure the charges were dismissed. He had been an innocent musician, she said, intent on playing music rather than protesting war.

Little John floated out of the courtroom and down the street with his chanting friends. They held hands and danced along the sidewalk, hair and fringes floating behind them.

"There's a lot of that going around these days," Shirley told Moon Rose.

"For sure," Moon Rose replied.

Moon Rose stayed in touch with Shirley until Shirley left Rolled, Smythe and Right to start her own practice. Until then, they watched over the wild and wandering young man, although he never seemed to have any awareness of their oversight. Shirley sent the draft board notice of John Finchley's registration at the University of Washington.

Fortunately for Little John, it was the age before computers. His file was buried with thousands of others in a military metal file cabinet and was never rechecked to see if he actually attended classes.

Chapter Five

Sara looked across the room where Philip scowled from the depths of an overstuffed chair, Big John glowered at her from the brown leather loveseat and Katy, leaning against the mahogany bar, pulled her lips and eyebrows together so tightly her face looked like a cloth purse puckered up against thieves.

It's the battle of the looks, Sara mused. What a terrible family we are. We belong in T.S. Eliot's Wasteland. *Affections lose their object... lodged in memory.* If love exists no longer it must die. Did it ever exist here?

Big John had widened with the years. He wore massive multi-colored shirts and wide, gray baggy trousers. As he widened, Katy shrank.

The reverse of Jack Sprat, Sara thought.

Mom can eat no fat. Mom has dwindled into a stick figure with a wire brush for hair. Piggy Philip has sucked her dry – not that there was so much moisture to start with.

Sara's gaze moved to her stepfather.

There is not much love there either, she thought. *In rats' alley... where the dead men lost their bones.* He has no substance, opinions mouthed for sound and fury. *The fragments of his old beliefs are shored against his ruin,* and he, inside that overstuffed body, is dry and turning to dust. What is he afraid of? Is it Little John? John is my soul. Or is it me?

"I am going to Seattle," she said flatly, enjoying the ripple of irritation she caused. "I have been accepted by the University of Washington in Seattle. I am going to live in Seattle. I want you to set up an account for me in a bank there."

Katy shifted uneasily. She didn't like the idea of Sara controlling money and living in another town.

Perhaps she should insist that Sara stay home, insist that Sara become a help around the house and wait for the right man to marry. That was the way things were supposed to be. But something about Sara bothered her. She had odd ideas.

Katy shrugged.

Big John nodded. He felt he had no choice. The girl's eyes were commanding. In any case, any member of his family, even if she was just a stepdaughter, should never appear to want for anything. At least she had some ambition, not like John. At least the girl had a sense of what other people might think of her, and through her, of him.

"How much money did you have in mind?" he asked.

Sara had already worked out her budget. She had called a school friend who was already at the university. Sara knew how much it would take to live luxuriously and decided to ask for more than double the amount. She figured that $125 a month would rent her a nice house in the University District; food would cost about $100—clothes, $100, and gas for her car $20. Another $100 would take care of any entertainment.

She knew how to get money from her stepfather. When she turned sixteen, she had appealed to his desire to look like a prosperous family man because she wanted a car. He gave her the $1,800 she needed for a new black TR-3 sports car. She drove it down the coast to school and back up to Abraham. In Seattle, she wanted the lifestyle to go with the car.

"I need about $2,500 a month," she said.

Big John blinked. That was more money than he paid his managers at the yard.

"You better learn to get by on $2,000 a month," he told her. "That's the limit."

She tilted her head. Her corn silk hair drifted across her cheekbone. Big John noticed again how beautiful she had become. Something caught in his chest. He swallowed it away.

"You'll pay for tuition and books?" she murmured.

He nodded.

"OK," she said. "I'm leaving tomorrow. Let me know tonight what bank to use. You make the arrangements this afternoon."

Then she left the room.

Philip made a disgusted sound. The girl was actually giving orders. How dare she?

Katy swallowed her disapproval by muttering "Good riddance" at the closing door.

Big John frowned slightly, shook his head and picked up his newspaper.

****

By the time the sun burned away the high summer clouds over the forest, Sara was driving through the mountains. By noon, she was heading inland, feeling the road along the Columbia River vibrating through the gas pedal, feeling the warm wind whip her hair behind her; watching the gleaming black hood push through tunnels and under steep banks. Then she was going north past old mills, brick factories and roads that went nowhere, where asphalt crumbled into tall dry grass crackling in the summer heat.

She knew she would find him in Seattle. He was somewhere there, playing music. Aunt Audrey's letter had arrived at her school while she was packing to come home after graduation. It had been a disturbing letter and the reason she decided to attend the University of Washington. Aunt Audrey had written:

You know he visited with me for a while after he got out of school and he seemed a little strange but he played the guitar so wonderfully. You should have heard him! He learned all the songs on our old 78s. Would you believe it? Anyhow, after that he left Abraham and said he was going back to Seattle.

I haven't heard from him since your Dad told the draft board where to find him but they rejected him. I was worried about him going. So many are being killed in the jungle these days. So I was glad they turned him down because they said he was in bad health and mentally unstable. But that worries me too.

Milly told Mitch and Mitch told my Gary that your Dad arranged for him to go to school and found him a place to stay. I hope he went there.

Gary sends his love. He is bearing up although he doesn't have that many good days now. But he always finds a way to smile.

I am glad to hear you are doing so well. Where have you decided to go to college? I know you will do fine whatever you decide.

Love always,
Aunt Audrey

Sara was tired by the time she reached Seattle so she booked into a motel in the University District, ate in a nearby diner and went to bed.

The next morning she registered for classes. The clerk behind the desk reminded Sara of a bank teller. She had brown beehive hair, black-rimmed glasses and she looked very bored.

"Please give me your Seattle address," the beehive said. "We don't have one listed for you. Are you staying in one of the dorms?"

Sara had an idea.

"I'm staying with my brother," she said. "His name is John Finchley."

"You are Sara Finchley?"

Sara nodded.

"Well, what is *that* address?" the clerk demanded.

Sara gave an embarrassed smile.

"Well, you see, I don't know. I've been away at boarding school and he sent me the address but I lost it. I thought maybe you could look it up for me."

The clerk's eyes narrowed. "I need more information about you before I can do that. Do you have any other identification?"

Sara produced her driver's license and pointed out that she had the same address as her brother in Abraham and that the law firm of Rolled, Smythe and Right handled the family's affairs.

The clerk picked up the telephone to call the admissions secretary and inclined her head at a row of hard wooden seats along the side of the room. "You'll have to wait there while they look that up. It may take a few minutes to verify all that information."

The body has a mind of its own but doesn't know which way it should go, Sara thought. *I know where I'm going. I know who's going with me. I know who I love, but the dear knows who I'll marry.*

****

"He ain't here! Go away!"

The apartment manager slammed the door. Sara felt like crying.

She stared at the painted wood for a few seconds and wondered what was wrong with the man. She walked away from the stone building and thought about Little John. She knew he was close, somewhere close; she could feel his soul, see his eyes.

Eyes I dare not meet in dreams, in death's dream kingdom.

The sun gleamed on the grass in front of the apartment building. She remembered the sunny days when they had crept below the bluffs, walked on rocks, ran through foam and lay beneath the shadow of the cliff.

A girl and boy, in our youth time had been, loving and feeling as the sea echoed green.

The sun did descend, and our sport had an end, a sister and brother were sent back for the rest and sport no more seen on the darkening green.

Sara saw a longhaired man carrying a guitar. A guitar! He might know where to find Little John.

She ran after him.

"Do you know of anybody up here who plays Sousa marches? He wears a monocle."

He grinned and flashed a row of white even teeth at her.

"Sure do," he replied cheerfully. "That would be Barefoot John. He hangs around the Aggervawn or at the Café Korner."

Sara resisted the urge to hug him.

"Where is that? Where is the Aggervawn?"

He pointed down the street.

"Six blocks that way. Four blocks left."

Sara walked down the avenue. She saw a bearded man in a tweed jacket with leather elbows and a long-haired woman standing before a store window. They were reflected against brightly patterned skirts and fringed shawls. Sara turned away from them and watched colors flow into the gutter and run bubbling down the drain. Their shapes cast a shadow over the flowing light.

It began to rain although the sky was still bright. Every drop glittered.

Then Sara was at the Aggervawn where, from the other side of the colored beads, Moon Rose swayed toward her. Candlelight shone through her kinky red hair and her eyes were dark jewels against the halo.

This flower woman is part of his world, Sara thought.

"Where is Barefoot John?" Sara asked. "He is my friend."

Moon Rose looked at her and nodded. She knew right away that this was somebody important to Barefoot John.

"He's probably in the park. He likes the chestnut trees this time of year and comes back with his pockets full of nuts."

"The park?"

"Volunteer Park, where they have the chestnut trees. They are full now of spiked nuts that fall as you walk away from the stone lions."

"Full now? Where?"

Moon Rose's finger pointed through the beads to the road outside where a bus waited against the curb.

"That will take you there. That will take you to the park."

"And the chestnut trees?"

"And the chestnut trees."

"He'll be there?"

"He'll be there and perhaps you can give him this," Moon Rose said, handing her a key. "It's time he got this back. It's the key to his place."

Sara took the key and ran out to catch the bus.

The windows streaked with rain. Bubbles formed, ran together and then sank. Sara stared at the flat, wet, green expanse of lawn in the park as the bus rolled to a stop. Clouds rolled back.

The sun came out. Sara found the stone lions and walked beneath the spreading chestnut trees until she reached the conservatory. He was there. She could feel him. The door closed behind her on the dank smell of earth in the glass house of plants. She looked at the blooming cactus plants and realized that she was finally free to make her own choices. She no longer needed to be judged by fellow students, teachers or her mother.

Sara smiled slightly, recalling that in the end, without breaking a single rule, without really being noticed, without ever making a close friend, she had emerged at the top of her class academically. Despite her teachers' uneasiness around her, their distrust of her controlled expression and her lack of childlike emotions – despite all that, they had to admit she had been a good, hard-working student, her grades were excellent and she should be given chance to go on in life. They never knew about the poetry that ran through her mind at every moment, her words and the words of writers from past centuries; the syllables in her mind forever singing.

The air in the greenhouse was tropical and scented with orchid ferns and bog grass.

And there he was, leaning over the pond watching the reflection of his hair, the reflection rippling with his hair. He was in the water. He was the water. He could not move because his face was looking back at him from under all those silver ripples in the muggy air.

She touched his shoulder and he stopped drowning.

He smiled across at her for they were the same height and she felt the warmth of his smile.

"Wow," he breathed. "You."

"Me," she said. "I came to find you."

Something under her heart tripped and fell.

The sun broke through another cloud as they walked across the emerald-tipped grass, back past the stone lions and to the street.

"I'm always lost," he said. "I couldn't find my classes."

She reached out to hold his hand.

"They've set us free," she said. "We don't have to find anything but ourselves."

He stopped walking and turned her to him. The clouds moved from the suns that were his eyes.

"No more smiling at the hens for you."

"No more marching behind tight asses for you."

He grinned then.

"I think I have a pad. But I couldn't find that either."

"I found it. Let's go there," she said.

They sat close beside each other on the bus, his guitar across their laps. They didn't talk but looked out the window at the flat gray sidewalk flowing past them and the water under the bridges. Finally, they left the bus in front of the red brick apartment building where he was supposed to live.

This time the apartment manager let her in. The lady lawyer had described John very well and had warned the manager that he might show up at any time. She made it clear that whether he showed up alone or with someone, he had to be admitted. Moreover, if he did show up, the manager was to call her. The information that this mysterious tenant was on the premises would earn the apartment manager an extra $50.

The manager led Sara and Little John to the neatly furnished apartment. Sara closed and locked the door behind them.

Little John looked around.

"This is a really straight pad," he said.

"It's yours," Sara told him. "We can make as crooked as you want."

Little John wandered into the bedroom. He took off his monocle. He took off his clogs. He put down his guitar and he pulled off his pants. He lay naked, spread-eagled on the white chenille bedspread.

"Come here," he said.

Sara took off her jeans, her shirt and her underpants and walked toward him like a pale and fluid statue. For a while, they were back on the sand, parallel figures, linked by shape, the outer edges of a mandala.

Later, Sara remembered and wrote in her journal:

Entwined, we see the same moonrise, gaze at ripples where there is no tide, and turn our forms to solid substance, as we love the laughing lotus.

Chapter Six

Sara blew on the window, making a mist. She drew two hearts on the pane. She took Lucy's finger and drew across the glass, saying as she moved Lucy's finger, "Mom loves Lucy."

Lucy whimpered. Sara brought her to her breast to feed.

A tendril grew in Sara's mind, drawing behind it a whole tree of knowledge, a whole garden of delight.

How tiny she was when she was born, Sara thought.

I was afraid to hold her. Her little hands curled like shells. We are an island now as I rock and hold her and she feeds from my breast. I rock her gentle in this old green rocker. We rock in the held-breath of not dark nights as street lights gleam on the peach trees growing from the sidewalk.

Her soft scent fills the night as she holds my nipple in her mouth, sucks the nipple, sucks from me my milk, my love, sucks out my heart so hard that seems it can never be complete without her.

Sara heard his voice in the living room where the band was wrangling over the songs they tuned their guitars to play but never seemed to finish. They were recording their music on a reel-to-reel tape player in front of the brick fireplace. Mattresses leaned up against the windows to muffle echoes.

I will never understand how Lucy can sleep through all that noise; the words, the songs, Little John's riffs, Cory's boom-boom bass guitar and Pierce beating on drums and scraping the washboard with metal finger picks.

He had been so wonderful when she was pregnant. They found the U-shaped cottage close to the university with a garden space enclosed by its wings and peach trees growing in the parking strip. It had an extra room for the child they were waiting for.

He called her swelling stomach, "Our beautiful balloon" and sang "Up, up and away!" each time he came home to kiss her.

He sang, "Up, up and away in my beautiful balloon!" as they wheeled her away to the delivery room in Northwest Hospital.

"Up, up and away!" it had been, for she was in labor for twenty-four hours and Lucy was born long after all the fluids had drained away and the pain was tearing her apart. They drugged Sara and slit her open and *into the dangerous world Lucy leapt, helpless naked, piping loud.*

After they were back home, the three slept in their "love balloon" nestled in the big bed, like three spoons, with Little John on the outside and Lucy cradled in Sara's arms.

The days blend with nights as bass notes blend in the blues haze, shaking the crystal beads, shuddering the tendrils of ivy twining along the window, trembling water in the sink full of dishes, Sara thought.

Hippie women in multi-colored skirts left the recording sessions in the living room and visited the nursery. They hovered over mother and daughter and clucked advice. Sara was uncomfortable.

Lucy sleeping does lay while the beasts of prey came from caverns and viewed the babe asleep.

How they stand around us as she lies in my arms, she thought. Those old ladies of the band have sideways, unsmiling stares.

I am not one of them. They can't understand that I do not smoke their pot or drink their wine because she is feeding below my heart and I want her food to be clear. They smoked and drank as their babies sucked so what is wrong with me?

****

The band learned enough songs to play gigs. Within six months, Sara was nursing Lucy under the stages of coffee houses. Above her, the platform rattled as Little John played.

Lucy slept through the music. By the time she was two, Lucy was put to bed on coats in musicians' rooms around Puget Sound as Sara clapped and John played.

Sara carried Lucy in a sling on the bus to Pike Market where she found fruit, fish and brown rice. They searched the musty antique shops along the seawall for small glass pill bottles Little John could slip over his middle finger. The resulting harmonics of his 12-string bottle-neck blues made audiences cheer and whistle. People filled his guitar case with coins when he played on street corners.

Sara took Lucy to a daycare center while she took English classes at the University, partly to keep money flowing from Abraham and because she loved the linguistically rich atmosphere of classes in ivy-covered Padelford Hall. Sara read the poetry she was studying to Lucy, made friends with poetry-minded graduate students and argued for hours over the origin of King Lear.

Everybody loved Little John. Students and instructors invited him to play at parties in rooftop penthouses where marijuana joints bristled from crystal holders. Little John sang and strummed for rapt, angular and acerbic wives of professors and for students who rolled out words like marbles to trip their listeners. Students and teachers danced and listened to Little John's music until the sun pinked the flat salt water beyond the docks. Sara sat on the outskirts thinking about T.S. Eliot.

Here we go round the prickly pear
Prickly pear prickly pear
Here we go round the prickly pear
At five o'clock in the morning.

John was the golden man. He laughed until his monocle fell out. His joy, as sweet as the white peaches outside, bubbled through their little house.

He wrote a song for her called "Sara's Song" rolling with riffs and rivulets of notes. He wrote another called "Lucy's Carpet Sleep"

inspired by Lucy's nap on the carpets stacked in the musicians'
room at the Aggervawn, where he still went to play.

Sara wrote in the pages of her journal:

The cosmic wind changed, grew sharper.

A man turned bird madly fights the coming wind, pushes beak to
puncture vacant sky, is trapped and never lands.

****

By the time she was three, Lucy was restless in the musicians'
rooms. She wanted to walk and talk and wriggle. Sara was not
content just to sit and applaud at the right times. She wanted to be
heard as well. Sara wanted to read her poetry, to be taken seriously.
More and more often, Sara stayed home with Lucy while Little John
went off to play.

Sara bought a mandolin and taught herself to play it. She thought,
perhaps, learning to play would help her be part of Little John's
music world. Other "old ladies" played guitar and mandolin. But
Little John had no patience with her fumbling untrained fingers and
while he let her strum with him a little, he soon would soar off on
his own clouds of sound far above her reach.

Sara knew she would never be able to join him so contented
herself by playing her mandolin for Lucy who was too young to
notice that her mother never learned how to tune it properly.

Leopards and tygers played around her as she lay, as her father
bow'd his mane and came to kiss her, but from his eyes of flame
ruby tears they came.

****

Little John wanted to take Lucy back to Abraham. He wanted to
confront the family with the glorious truth of his child.

"We can show them!" he said. "We are a real family."

Sara refused. There would be no acceptance there, she knew, just contempt and condemnation.

"We can never let them know," she said. "They'll see Lucy as a disgrace. They will not accept you as her father. You're my stepbrother."

"Incest is best," he muttered in his recently acquired British Beatle-type accent. "But this ain't even incest. We're not related. It's not like I'm the Philip Man, your true step-bro'. I'm not really related by either blood or soul to that Stone woman – am I love!"

"You know they don't care what the reality is. They only care about how things look!" Sara snapped. "Especially your father. They'll force me to move home and they'll take Lucy away. Look what they did to us when we were kids. Do you want Lucy in a boarding school like we went to? Besides, they'll stop sending me money for my expenses at school. They could also stop Shirley from sending you money. Then we'll both have to get real jobs."

Little John slapped his forehead.

"Ah no! Not that!"

Sara giggled.

Sara liked keeping their world a secret. She liked floating through the seasons on music and poetry, fueled by pot and a little acid. Little John was happy and while he also liked getting stoned and said acid greased his creativity, he was not totally zoned out every day.

His band called themselves "Acid Flash". They played jug band music, blues and sitar harmonics. Little John said the best place to be a musician was in Seattle.

"Way better than Los Angeles."

Rev. Gary Davis was cruising the West Coast, sliding his bottle back and forth on twelve vibrating strings.

"Pure Religion!" he sang.

"Groovy!" cried Little John.

But as Little John began to go to more and more gigs without Sara and Lucy, Sara felt more left out.

Sara thought it was as if, having made himself a baby, Little John felt he didn't have to anything else. He had her. He had a child. The two were conveniently parked at home but a hindrance in public. At the same time, Sara needed him more than ever. Her world turned to quicksand. She lost her bearings, her self-reliance. She felt that in John's eyes she was an extension of Lucy, not a real person.

John did not want to be needed. He wanted to concentrate on his music and the new friends who hung with Pierce and Cory. Back to being Barefoot John, wreathed in pot smoke, he was fading back into the elusive wanderer he had had been before and she could not stop him.

John's new friends were not easy around her. It seemed that after the Vietnam War ended, paranoia grew and a kind of barefoot snobbery emerged. Sara was too full of ideas, scraps of poetry and herself. She was aloof from the women and her bland blue eyes unnerved them. Barefoot John was their hero; he was the artist. She was merely his old lady.

The band bought more equipment, more speakers; acquired more wires, guitars and old ladies. John purchased a van that doubled as a sleeping area once the equipment was unloaded. Acid Flash accepted more gigs out of town. There was no room for Sara and Lucy in the van so they stayed home.

John and the band were gone for days at a time and Sara was alone with Lucy, often more miserable than she thought anybody could be.

Up, up and away... but to where?

Lucy grew quickly and spoke without a trace of a childish lisp. Each evening, rather than children's stories, Sara read her poems by William Blake, Gertrude Stein or T.S. Eliot.

Sara found comfort in the sound of words and the songs in the syllables. Lucy seemed to understand everything.

Sara felt Lucy would get more out of books if she learned to read them herself so she taught the four-year-old to read and write. Lucy made a crayon drawing for the refrigerator with "A ROSE IS A ROSE IS A ROSE" shaped in clumsy purple letters.

John thought Sara was pushing Lucy. Reading too early would cause Lucy problems in school, he said.

"You've made her different. They won't like her to be smarter than the others."

"But she is already different and smarter." Sara said.

The nights were dark and long. Now, when he came back, he crawled into bed, rolled over and slept. He became a void in the darkness, a lonely place she should not touch. So Sara lay staring at the ceiling.

Once, when she was groggy and light-headed from flu, she asked him to stay home, to please stay home, to be with her, to stay home and hold her. She needed his touch.

"You have no right to ask me this," he said.

Then he said, "You don't believe in my music."

He went off into the night as she coughed behind the lump in her throat.

Which of his friends said that? Sara wondered.

She didn't ask him to stay with her again.

Two weeks later, she asked if they could go somewhere together as family, just the three of them. He agreed because no gigs were scheduled for that Saturday. Sara packed a picnic lunch and they drove to Copalis Beach on the ocean. Sara thought that there, where the waves roared, she could explain to him that she wanted more out of life. She would suggest that perhaps he could look for a job in a record store or something. Perhaps he could be made to understand how much she needed him around.

As Lucy played in the surf, Sara tried to talk to Little John but started to cry when she tried to explain how much she loved him. His eyes clouded because she was saying that he should not keep moving on from gig to gig. She wanted him to stay and conform to something that was not his idea.

"If you're so miserable, call your Mother. You can take Lucy to visit her," he said.

"How can I do that?" Sara cried. "You know I can't do that!"

His eyes drifted off. She was cluttering his mind with something heavy. Not good.

"They'll find out sooner or later. You should visit your mother."

"No, I can't!" she cried, her voice almost as high as the sea gull screeching overhead. "I can't! They must never know about Lucy! We won't get any money to live on!"

Lucy came back from the ocean's edge and they had their lunch without speaking. Then he lifted Lucy to his shoulders and ran to the surf, the sun behind him, becoming a moving totem pole with a bird on top. Lucy's arms were its wings. Lucy was flying.

"Up, up and away!" he sang.

****

Lucy walked along the sand.

Mom and Dad were talking loudly. The wind blew the waves into little foamy spikes. The water tickled her feet and made her ankles numb. Then she started running and her feet felt fine. She ran along the gritty cold sand and jumped over the white lines of foam that spread around her.

There was a bird high in the sky, wheeling and crying out. She could still hear what Mom and Dad were saying.

"We can't tell them!"

Her mother's voice was high and shrill and carried above the waves and the wind sound.

Her father's voice was lower so Lucy heard only some of the words.

"Why not? They should know."

"We can't!" her mother cried again but the bird drowned out the next part so Lucy heard only the word "Money!" before the wave foam splashed around her ankles and rose to her knees. The sand sucked at her feet. Perhaps it would pull her away into the green palace of mermaids.

She ran back to them. The sand was warm between her toes.

Mom had egg sandwiches and little chocolate cakes in the basket. She had real lemonade in a jug. It was cold and sour and sweet all at the same time. Then Dad, breaking away from the funny silence growing around them, took her up high on his shoulders and went bouncing and running and jumping over the water while Mom lay down on the blanket to hide her face.

Dad was singing beneath her. His voice rose with the sound of the wind, the waves and the calling bird wheeling above them. She felt like a bird with feathers flying high into the wild and wonderful sky on Dad's strong shoulders.

Chapter Seven

Sara gazed numbly at the paper in her hands. What could she do now? He was gone, off with his band, running from her and Lucy. They had argued before he left for the gig. They often argued these days. She was becoming more rooted. He was growing larger wings, becoming restless. Lucy hovered between them like a small shiny chain keeping him to her, anchored to the home and the ground. The chain was breaking. The circle was breaking.

I GOTTA GO
KISS LUCY
I WOKE UP THIS MORNING
LOOKIN FOR MY WALKIN SHOES
IT'S ALL RIGHT
DON'T KNOW WHEN I'LL BE BACK
JOHN

That was it. He would not be back. Damn! Damn! He couldn't even tell me in real words. He had to echo! Damn Dylan! Damn Robert Johnson! Damn them all!

Sara paced the room alone, smoothed her hair with an unsteady hand and put another record on the player. Janice Joplin screamed.

What now? What now?

The next days ran one into the other without shape or sound. Sara took Lucy to the daycare center. Sara went to her classes. Sara read her assignments. Sara sat quietly. Sara felt nothing. She wondered why she did not feel a great tearing grief, a great dramatic emotion, why she did not paint her cheeks with ash or drive desperately to Portland. She felt deadened as if he had taken her soul with him and she was not really alive at all.

Her spirit was under a stage somewhere, vibrating to the sound of his heels drumming to the rhythms of the blues.

Finally, she decided do something about her numbness so she took Lucy to Volunteer Park, thinking that the damp smell in the conservatory would bring her feelings back. The park was not what it had been. The lions looked like tombstones, the grass like the rolling slopes of a cemetery. All around her were people dressed in black, walking solemnly along the flat gray paths. Under the pallid sky, there was no laughter. William Blake's words filled her mind.

So I turn'd to the Garden of Love
That so many sweet Bowers bore
And I saw that it was filled with graves
And tombstones where flowers should be
And Priests in black gowns, were walking their rounds,
And binding with briars, my joys and desires

****

Sara asked Marla, the wildest woman in her Sylvia Plath seminar to come over and get stoned. She sat with Marla on the living room floor, swallowing pills and drinking. The next night, Marla brought more people to join the party.

Lucy woke in the night screaming with fear but by then the house was full of people and noise. Nobody heard her so she stumbled into the cloud of smoke.

Lucy struggled against the strangers' hands and the noisy music scared her. Then, wrapped in a blanket and weary, she thought it best to sulk upon her mother's breast.

In a few weeks, Sara found that her income, which before had isolated her from the other students, now brought people to her home in droves as she supplied them with the highs and lows they needed.

John did not call, write or come back, although Moon Rose at the Aggervawn told Sara where Acid Flash was playing. They had been cast as a band in a western movie filmed along the Oregon coast and they performed at a mini-Woodstock in Hoquiam. Moon Rose told Sara that Little John had a new girlfriend, a redhead.

****

"Of course she's a redhead!" Sara told Marla. "He particularly liked redheads. His favorite groopies were redheads."

Marla stretched out her black mesh legs and murmured, "You're not a redhead."

"I should have been," Sara muttered.

They were in the backyard. Lucy was arranging large Legos into orderly and colorful ranks on the damp grass. The sky was deep blue, a color unusual for Seattle and what usually would have filled Sara with joy. This morning, however, she did not pay attention. The sky was the sky and her head ached. Traffic droned along the street.

Muffled sounds of an argument came from the house next door.

"What do you mean?" Marla asked.

"Redheads are independent, feisty and good in bed," Sara said. "At least that's what they say. And I am all of those."

"You are?" Marla replied doubtfully.

"Don't you believe me?" Sara carefully pulled a blade of grass from its green socket and chewed on the tender white end.

"Shit. All you do is go to classes, read and take care of a baby. That's not very independent. And you haven't fucked anyone since your old man left. Shit, you're no redhead. You're just a broken-hearted blond."

Sara glared at Marla and then giggled. Her friend was outspoken and often rude but did not hide her opinions behind a fake pleasant expression.

Marla also had a deep voice, not the high, trilling tone of most granola mamas wafting through the U-district. Sara liked that too.

"So what do you suggest?"

"DO something!"

Sara looked over at Lucy who had built a small tower of red, white and blue Legos.

Do something, Sara thought. I should. I should get a job and support Lucy on my own. If I was independent, I could take Lucy back to Abraham to visit Aunt Audrey if I wanted to.

"OK, OK," Sara said. "I have potential. I think."

"So work on it."

A door slammed next door. A child began to scream.

"Love in the city," Marla said.

****

The bald man leaned on his elbows and propped his chin on hairy hands. He had a large nose, narrow lips and a receding hairline. Sara could read nothing in his eyes. His controlled smile separated flaccid cheeks.

"Have you ever worked in an office?" he asked.

"No. But I type well, have a Master's in English and can work hard."

His eyes flicked down to her resume neatly squared off on the glass-topped desk.

"You have a child."

She nodded.

"No husband?"

She shook her head.

He leaned back in his chair and surveyed her with an expression both curious and disgusted.

"And you expect to work for a reputable firm?"

She nodded.

His smile broadened like a crack in an ice flow. He chuckled as if they were sharing a special secret.

"I don't think you would be suitable for our operation. Unwed mothers of children don't have the commitment to the firm we require. But you don't need to worry. You are a good-looking woman. You'll soon find some man who would be happy to take care of you and your child."

He looked at her expectantly. She said nothing. Then he leaned forward and lowered his eyes. Sara felt as if a curtain dropped and a pit opened beneath her feet.

"I'm sorry," he said.

Sara went back outside to walk the cement to her next interview.

More weeks passed, Sara could not find any work. Her depression only lifted when Marla brought friends over for parties.

Eyes I dare not meet in dreams
In death's dream kingdom
These do not appear...

Why has all the joy blown away? Sara wondered. Am I that weak, that wind-dried?

More people came over. The party went on and on. There seemed to be no point for her to attend classes. Too many words overflowed her mind. Pills overflowed her mind. One night a visiting rock band set up in the living room. The little house was swollen with strange people and filled with the smells of patchouli oil, pot and soup. Lucy tried to find Sara but there was too much smoke so she went to sleep in her bedroom closet because it was quieter in there and seemed safer.

The noise disturbed the neighbors. They called the police. The police found pot and pills and Lucy whimpering in the closet. Everybody was arrested and Lucy was taken away by Child Protective Services. Sara was locked in a cell above the King County Courthouse.

Katy and attorneys, Benjamin Rolled and George Right came to see her. By then, Shirley had left the firm and knew nothing about Sara's predicament. Sara faced the lawyers and her furious mother alone.

Big John was away on business. He did not want to see the girl in this state. How could she have had a baby? He thought she was smarter than that. Katy could handle that. He was more worried about his oldest son. Those damn lawyers had lost track of him again.

Sara would not tell them the name of Lucy's father. She huddled in her gray prison dress behind the glass in the visiting area and glared at the group clustered around the telephone on the other side

"No," she told them. "No! It doesn't matter. I won't tell you!"

Katy screwed up her lips. The lawyers frowned.

They left.

Sara's cellmates were sad and tough but were kind to her. Many of them had lost their children. They understood how she felt and told her that she probably would never see Lucy again.

The lawyer, George Right, came back the next day to talk to her before her arraignment.

"Where's Lucy?" Sara demanded.

Right sighed and handed her a sheet of paper and a pen.

"We found out who your child's father is," he said, almost sadly.

"How?"

"Hospital records, you have the same last name. Neighbors. The usual way."

"Where is she? Is she OK?"

Right handed Sara a sheet of paper.

"She's fine. You need to sign this," he said.

She read quickly.

"No!" she cried.

"This can keep you out of jail," Right said. "The prosecuting attorney has agreed to suspend your sentence if you sign this agreement and spend six months in a rehabilitation center. Once you complete your treatment, your case will be dismissed. If you don't agree, you will be charged with a felony and you may face a jail sentence. Unless you sign this, no family members will be available to take care of your little girl while you are in prison and she will be placed in foster care."

"No!"

"I'm afraid that is the way it is. Your mother will not acknowledge the child because of your relationship with the father. She wants the child out of the family's life. She believes the perception will be that the child was born from incest."

"But he's not my real brother!" Sara cried. "We're not really related at all!"

"Your mother believes in the importance of appearances," Right said. "At the same time, the boy's father believes in the importance of the family line. This document is a compromise."

"Not for me!"

"If you sign this, your daughter will be well taken care of until the father comes into his inheritance. Then, he can decide what to do with her. If you do not sign this, the court will take custody of her and she will be raised by foster parents. You will be disowned by your mother and will have to fend for yourself.

"If you sign this, you know your daughter will be safe, the family will make sure she is taken care of and then, in time, the father will regain custody."

"Can I see her again?"

Right shook his head.

"Not until the father is given custody. Then it will be up to him. This agreement was insisted upon by your parents. The alternative is to let your child be handled by the system. In addition, your parents will not pay for your time in a rehabilitation center. You would have to pay for it yourself or use welfare funds that you would have to pay back once you found work. Then, if you find a job and prove yourself reliable, you could petition to regain custody. Of course, foster care can be harmful and there are often problems."

"Problems?" she asked.

"It is a flawed system; sometimes state-paid foster parents are not good parents, and it may take some time for you to find work and prove to the court that you can take care of the child. That process can take years and is not always successful.

"Under this agreement, your father requires that the child is cared for comfortably, even luxuriously. We know of an exclusive boarding school that will shelter and nurture your little girl until her father is found and makes a decision about her future. Your father will pay for any therapy you need and all your expenses as you continue with your education. At the same time, your mother insists that you do not have contact with the child and do not claim custody until the father is placed in charge of his trust. At that point, if the father so chooses, you can all be together again. She cannot stop that."

"When will that be?"

"When the father turns thirty-five or if he becomes gainfully employed and proves reliable before then."

"He's a musician. You people don't think that is gainfully employed and he won't be thirty-five for years! Does John know about this?"

Right sighed.

"We seem to have lost track of him."

"Lost track! What about Shirley?"

"She's left the firm."

Sara buried her head in her hands. What could she do? She knew how hard it would be to find a job, especially if she had a prison record. She knew what happened to children in foster care. She remembered her days in boarding school. They weren't that bad.

"Are you trying to find him?"

"We are."

"Did you ask about the band in Portland? It was called Acid Flash. Did you ask his aunt, Aunt Audrey?"

"The aunt hasn't heard from him for a long time. The band broke apart several months ago. The other members we found don't know where he went. They said he might have gone to California. We are still looking."

Sara nodded. Gone, he was gone. He was flying on pills and pot. She knew how time could pass like that. She had been there. But he might land, remember her and Lucy and try to find them.

"What if he comes back looking for me?"

"We'll know. We'll explain what's going on and perhaps he'll make some changes so he can get custody of your daughter."

Sara looked at the document. Her throat hurt. "If I sign this, you say I won't go to jail. Lucy will be taken care of and I can finish school, perhaps start a career. Perhaps Little John will turn his life around and we will be a family again."

"Perhaps." Right smiled stiffly. "You are young. There is always hope. You can go on with your life. After you have been treated for your er – problem – you will be sent to college in Canada. You can start over where nobody knows you. Meanwhile, your child will be well cared for."

Sara's brain whirled. She felt sick. How could she not see Lucy? Not hold her? But what choice did she have? At least, this way, Lucy would be safe from abuse. And perhaps Little John would do something. He was the one who wanted to take Lucy home. Oh, how she wished she had listened to him.

How could she have let Lucy see the parties, breathe the smoke, be there, be found like that, hiding in a closet? How could she have done those things?

Sara knew they were right. She had been an unfit mother. She drew the paper towards her. Right watched her impassively.

She shaped the signature but could not see her hand moving because her tears blurred everything.

Right took the signed document and left.

The arraignment went as smoothly as Right predicted. Sara left the courthouse and was taken straight to a treatment center.

Before she left, Right asked her if she knew anybody who could go through her belongings at the little house and select the things she wanted to store.

Sara shook her head. Her friends were facing legal issues of their own or were in hiding.

"Pack up Lucy's toys and clothes, so she has those with her," she said. "Ask one of your assistants, or somebody, to pack me a suitcase with a couple of changes of clothes and my poetry journal. It's in the drawer in the bedside table. Give everything else to the Goodwill."

Right remembered that John was a musician.

"Aren't there any musical instruments you want to keep? Or books?"

Sara thought about her mandolin and decided she never wanted to see it again.

"John has everything he needs, wherever he is. I can always buy more books."

During sessions at the rehabilitation center, she read her poems to the therapists who nodded and smiled.

Her need to see Lucy ate at her heart. Tears drenched her pillow each night. During the day she was calm and appeared as if she wanted to go on with her life. Her therapists were impressed.

After a while, she stopped crying at night. She stopped feeling emotion during the day. Perhaps it was the medication they gave her. Perhaps the poetry she wrote helped bury her pain.

After six months, she left the center and took a taxi to the airport. She was registered at McGill University in Montreal, Quebec, Canada, as far from the Northwest as the lawyers and her mother could place her, without crossing an ocean.

Sara wrote in her journal as the plane flew over Mount Rainer and across flat, white prairies to the St. Lawrence River.

I had a child in my neat house of dreams
Covering my eyes from graffiti everywhere
And living poetry of now
Whirling, they live on below.
ME
Above
ME
In pretentions of sanity
I grab one hurtling by in redacid limbo
Long hair flaying in voodoo beat
Tell me
What is it flying by?
The world whirling wait I am not old yet
Years days minutes second best left
Alone in the legions grabbing my reaching hands
Don't bring me DOWN baby
But baby
  Up
   Up
    And AWAY

She must be reaching for me now

Needing me

Her eyes tearful now
The big is too much
I can't touch her head
Knowing that
The big is too much
For even me

A soul I lost
Once wandering in the rain
Watching drops fall

And down below gray clouds
Somewhere a baby waits

I am alone I hear no sound
And even waves can't reach me now.

Chapter Eight

It was almost closing time in the bar under the Seattle viaduct. Outside were shadows in the mist, pounding waves, sounds of horns and sirens, and the smell of rotting wood.

Philip Finchley overflowed his chair. His voice rose as he stared at the man opposite him. The man's eyes flicked back and forth.

"The only way I can get the money is if that son-of-a-bitch is dead before he's thirty-five. Then it's all mine," Philip said, drumming his pudgy fingers on the cracked Formica.

The man held up a claw-like hand.

"Stop," he uttered. "Enough."

Philip shook his head from side to side.

"I know. I know. But can you help me?"

The man sighed heavily. Customers always sounded like children, waiting for him to pull them out of the swamp their own lives had created.

"You will pay half now," he said.

Philip pulled out a checkbook.

The man reared back.

"Not here, not by check," he hissed. He leaned forward, the sinews of his neck taut.

"Outside and in cash."

Philip closed his eyes and nodded.

"I thought you might want cash. I brought it. Then what happens?"

"I'll call you."

Philip looked warily at the bartender who was ignoring them and wiping down the counter so Philip stood up and walked out. As he opened the door, the night fog flowed into the room like oily water.

A few minutes later, the other man followed him.

The bartender began to wash glasses.

Two women held each other up as they were pushed inside by a cloud of opaque air.

"Two beers, Bud," one slurred.

The expressionless bartender turned towards the tap.

"Now your old man's coming back tomorrow," the speaker said to her companion. "Watcha gonna do? He'll want to know what you did with all the money he sent you. You told him you was getting teeth. You said you would get yourself all dolled up for him."

"I did not."

"You did. I was there. He said before he left he couldn't stand the way you looked no more. Think of the poor guy. He's been at sea six months. He'll want a good time."

"I'll give it him. He won't notice nothing."

"If you don't. Others will."

There was a silence.

"I'll remember who said that. Anyhow, I'll make him so happy, he'll forget my teeth."

"Ha! Forget! Yeah right!"

The bartender brought over foam-brimmed glasses.

"Last call, ladies," he said. "Last call. Goodnight."

****

There were rats in the corners of the abandoned warehouse. Little John didn't care because the rain could not reach him as he lay on his sleeping bag where stuffing leaked out in marshmallow puffs.

They are going to tear the building down, building down, building down, he sang in his head.

He sniffed. Everything smelled moldy.

I am mold, I am old, he thought.

He looked across the room at the doorway as she pulled aside the blanket nailed across it and came in. She had once been a girl, he thought. Now she was something else, something all tired and used up. She had soup in a Styrofoam cup. Her dark-circled eyes were lifeless.

"They sold the Café Korner," she said. "It's Indian food now. They don't speak much English. All they gave me was some leftover soup."

He struggled to a sitting position.

"Indian is good," he croaked.

He grinned through the hair that straggled down his cheeks revealing the few yellow teeth left in his mouth.

"It's OK, Koozie. OK. We'll get in the groove soon."

"The Aggervawn is closed too," she said. "But they still have musicians playing at Pike Market."

"Groovie."

"You gotta get better."

"I'll be fine. Koozie. Don't worry."

His hands shook as he held the cup to his mouth. A string of green cabbage fell from his mouth and draped itself on his beard.

She slid down the wall beside him and sat crossed-legged on the dust.

A pale gleam of sunlight pushed its way through a cracked window pane. It crossed the room and illuminated the guitar case and backpack in the corner furthest from them, stashed so they would not be contaminated by his vomit.

"Did you find Cory?" he asked.

She nodded.

"He was still at his mom's place, like you said."

"I figured he'd go take care of his Mom after he left the band. Acid Flash broke up after that."

"Why did it?" she asked.

He shrugged.

"It wasn't cool any more. Bye, Bye Miss American Pie." He paused and grinned again. "The day the music died."

She didn't seem to understand. She didn't know much of anything. Still, he was glad he knew her. She'd helped him get to Seattle and finally to this crash pad that he'd once known as a party pad. She was a good Koozie.

"That Cory's pretty straight. He said he knew where this place was and he'd come see ya tomorrow. He's playing a gig at something called Bumbershit or somethin' today. His old lady's a drag. You look like shit."

The world tipped around him. The soup tasted terrible. He struggled to his feet and stumbled to a hole in the floor where there once had been a toilet and threw up.

"You're awful sick," she said. "You need a doctor."

"Bad drugs. Bad cess," he muttered.

She stood up.

"I can't hang with you like this. I gotta get on with my own space," she told him. "That Cory will be here tomorrow. I gotta ago."

He nodded. The world faded into gray fuzz and mist as he teetered back to his sleeping bag.

"Shit," she said and went out the door.

Once outside, she looked back at the crumbling building and grimaced. She felt bad. She'd thought something was not right when the weird guy at her corner in Portland gave her two grams of coke for free and paid her $100 to make sure Barefoot got it.

Good thing she didn't do coke, she thought. She'd never liked the way it made her feel and she'd seen too many people spend all their money on it before they overdosed.

She thought maybe that's what had made Barefoot sick, even it didn't seem like a regular overdose.

The more Barefoot snorted, the sicker he got. He seemed to know something bad was happening because he told her to get him to Seattle, no matter what.

Barefoot's not a bad guy, she thought sadly. She didn't think he'd get much further.

There was a telephone booth on the corner. She dialed zero.

"There's a guy in the old warehouse by uum – the last big dock. He's real sick," she told the operator and hung up. She walked up broken bricks to the city. Another town, other Johns, she thought.

The operator had received similar calls from that neighborhood. She called the police. They asked the two officers on duty in the area to check the warehouses along the block.

Meanwhile, Little John stirred, crawled out of the sleeping bag and pulled himself across the room to get to his backpack. He fumbled inside it and found a notepad and a pencil. He began to write. His hand wanted to shake more than he would let it.

This is the hardest song I ever played, he thought, as he formed one trembling letter at a time.

LUCY IN THE SKY
ARE YOU IN THE SKY? WITH DIAMONDS?
ITS DARK HERE. I WILL NEVER SEE YOU AGAIN
I SEE YOU SMALL AND GOLDEN RUNNING
I AM GOING SOMEWHERE
I WILL TRY TO FIND YOU SOMEHOW
MY GIRL, MY DAUGHTER MY ONLY CHILD
I LOVE YOU TELL YOUR MOTHER
TELL YOUR MOTHER
MY SARA
I
LOVE L YOUR DAD DAD DAD
BAREFOOT JOHN

JOHN FINCHLEY JR
TO LUC LUCY L
OVE

He pushed the paper into the pack and, then on his belly, made it back to the sleeping bag where he passed out.

The police officers found him an hour later, winced at the stink, checked his pockets for identification, found nothing and called the paramedics. One officer stood outside the building, waiting for the ambulance.

The other stood by the window, shining his flashlight on Little John whose body hung to life by barely visible breaths. Little John's mind was filled with sand shapes in triangles and patterns, coming and going around him, flowing below him in the surf. He flew with wind birds, landing for brief seconds on rocky ledges.

The sun set. The paramedics hurried to put him on a stretcher, get him out of the smell and dust and rush him to Soundview Hospital on the hill above the city.

Nobody noticed the guitar case and backpack in the darkest corner. They stayed hidden until the next morning when Cory poked his head into the doorway. He called Little John's name and waited for a few minutes but his friend had traveled beyond the sound of any human voice.

Cory wandered around the room, tripped over the guitar case and saw the pack.

These are his, Cory thought. He'll be back to get them. That why he sent that girl. I better keep them for him. He knows where to find them.

Cory took the guitar and pack home with him. Little John's stuff; the letter, his tapes, papers and treasures, once again were somewhere safe.

****

A whale sent foam into a white sky. Little John ran with sandpipers down to the shore, drawn by pulsing waves and the outline of a boat against the flat black horizon.

The birds made clouds of feathers as he flew with them and plunged into the blue, glittering sea, down to the bright sun, white light, hanging and singing below. He swam, laughing as the notes rang through him, through him and out into the dark night, the white light and the great big... big....

"He's gone," the nurse said.

The paramedic was not surprised. "They don't last long."

"You find any identification?"

"Nope."

"Bye, bye John Doe," the nurse said sadly. "Under that dirt he didn't look very old."

"He wasn't," the paramedic said. "You can tell by the feet. I bet he wasn't much past thirty."

Chapter Nine

Although years had passed since Shirley left Rolled, Smythe and Right and had any contact with the Finchleys, she never forgot them. Images of the strange little family haunted her dreams.

She now practiced law in Seattle and often wondered if her choice to move there had something to do with them.

"You're still hoping to run into them," her roommate and best friend, Phyllis Murphy, said.

Phyllis was as small as Shirley was large. Phyllis taught English at several community colleges. She called herself a "freeway flyer" because, despite her poetry, her doctorate, her Guggenheims and her Fulbright; her strange mix of stubborn dogma, extreme talent and belligerent appeals for the underdog kept her from landing a full-time, permanent, tenure-track position.

Shirley first met Phyllis at a poetry reading given by one of Shirley's clients. He had been charged with making obscene calls after a woman turned him in for reading his work to her over the telephone.

Shirley's first impression of Phyllis was of an annoying little woman, draped by a white lace shawl, who stood up and asked the client about his lack of sensibility and lack of respect for women in general.

"How can you continue to write about the subversion of woman to man by giving validity to that word fuck? It's like a gunshot or a hit. It has nothing to do with love or union," Phyllis demanded.

Shirley's client could not think of a response so he ignored her and acknowledged another member of the audience. That person wanted to know where he got his inspiration for poems.

"That's a much easier question to fuckin' answer," the client replied.

Later, during the reception, Shirley tried to defend the man.

"He has the right to write about what he likes," she told Phyllis.
"I have right to say what I think about it," Phyllis replied.
Shirley laughed. "So you do."

Shirley thought later that was when her opinion changed and the friendship began. They found they liked the same type of theater and the same type of art. The next week, they went to a reading by Ursula Le Guin and listened to a minimalistic concert featuring crystal glasses hammered unevenly by black-garbed, unisex musicians.

Odd, but interesting, they agreed, over fried prawns at The Saigon in Seattle's International District.

While Shirley struggled to find clients for her new practice, Phyllis' landlord raised her rent. Phyllis moved in with Shirley and sorted out Shirley's clutter of paper, food droppings and half-finished projects. Phyllis decorated the fifth-floor apartment with delicate drapes, beads and Japanese prints.

Phyllis talked to Shirley about ideas and issues. Shirley was happy to listen. Her job involved with more depressing conversations since, as she told Phyllis, her cases were primarily in the "D" category – divorces, drunks and delinquents.

"It's still not as depressing as watching a rich family eat its young, like guppies in a small fish tank," Shirley said, thinking about the Finchleys. She reminded herself that Little John had been assigned to Felix Oswood at Rolled, Smythe and Right and that she should focus on her "D" business. The Finchleys were not her concern any more.

*****

She finally met Felix Oswood beside her at the buffet table during a Law Society dinner.

Oswood placed the head of a shrimp in his mouth and bit it gingerly so Shirley could see the blood-red cocktail sauce ooze from his puffed lips. Oswood was chinless, with tufts of red hair leaping from his scalp like the bristles of a toothbrush. He had no eyebrows.

Shirley smiled at him politely, noting his politically correct slender frame.

He runs because it has to be done, does not smoke and never laughs spontaneously, she thought. Oswood saw her and his expression changed. He knew who she was. For some reason, he suddenly felt he had to explain something.

"Hi," Oswood mumbled through his shrimp-filled mouth. "You used to handle that Finchley boy, didn't you?"

Shirley nodded. This is strange, she thought.

"How is he?" she asked politely.

"Not a clue," Oswood told her. "Last seen somewhere in Portland, stoned to the gills, years ago."

"You still paying his bills?" Shirley asked.

Oswood grabbed another shrimp and immersed its head in the cocktail sauce as he spoke.

" Nothing's come in for him for a very long time. We're still sending money to the girl and her mother."

"You don't know where he is?"

"He knows where to find us if he wants to." Oswood said. He slurred his words slightly. He had been visiting the no-host bar for a while.

Shirley frowned, feeling a stab of worry. "Doesn't the family want to know where he is?"

Oswood shrugged. "They don't care. I don't think they want him messing around with them. In any case, the longer he is out of sight, the more the brother can control the old man – and his money."

And the more you buzzards can charge the family for doing nothing, Shirley thought.

"How's the little girl?' she asked.

Oswood bit apart another shrimp.

"They took the kid away after the mother, his sister, whatever, got caught up in the drug scene and heavy-duty partying. The cops raided her house and arrested everybody. The family, especially that old she-dragon mother, decided the kid was a shameful item and shipped her off to a very religious boarding school. I think they hoped that the father's influence and the kid's kind of incestuous origin would be prayed out of her. Oh yeah, they sent the girl to be bathed in the blood of the lamb for perpetuity. Amen"

He giggled.

"And the mother, Sara?" Shirley was starting to feel ill.

"We gave her the choice of going to jail, being disowned, losing family funding and having the kid raised by the state. Or she could agree to give up contact with the child until the father came into his inheritance and then he could take custody. She agreed to the latter. After all, she was in no shape to take care of the kid, the father was nowhere in sight and her old life was over. The kid is better off without her."

"What did the Sara do then?"

"She went into treatment and then to Montreal to McGill University to finish her studies and to make a new start as far away from the family as possible."

Shirley wondered why Oswood was telling her so much. In addition to the shrimp, she smelled the whisky on his breath. He was obviously drunk but there was something about this case that was bothering him, bothering him a whole lot.

Suddenly, Oswood seemed to realize he had been been indiscreet. He moved away from her and disappeared into the crowd, still clutching a shrimp.

****

That evening, back in the apartment, Shirley told Phyllis what he
had said.

"There's more to it all."

"What?"

"I don't know. Something."

"You could call that Moon Rose person."

"I tried this afternoon. The number has been disconnected."

"What does it worry you? You're not on the case any more."

Shirley looked out of the lead-squared window. It was raining.
She rubbed her fingertips on her hair.

"Perhaps because he was my first real case. And there was
something special about him. He was very talented."

Phyllis studied her friend.

"You need to think about this. Let's go on a trip."

"Where?"

"To the ocean. To the spirit beach at La Push."

"Spirit beach?"

"You'll see."

Shirley nodded. Phyllis knew these things.

Little John's world began against the rolling tides, she thought.
Perhaps the waves would tell her what to do or help her let go of the
image of the wandering boy who played a twelve-string guitar,
loved "groovies" and hardly ever wore shoes. She remembered
seeing a photograph of a Haida mask called the Shaman Returned. It
had reminded her of him, the world seen through one normal eye
and through a glass darkly with the other.

****

La Push was a Quileute Indian reservation with a motel and
cabins on the rocky northwest coast. The Quileute had settled among
the wind-bent trees after a volcano and floods drove them south

from Alaska, long before white people brought the diseases that wiped out the Northwest Indian civilizations.

Shirley and Phyllis decided to spend two days and nights listening to the ocean's roar where, according to legend, the First People landed their canoes.

The motel was right on the beach. Its windows fronted the ocean. By the time they settled in, the sun was a red ball slipping into gold-streaked surf.

"At the edge of the sea, all things seem to be connected," Shirley said. "At work, there are so many details, so much stuff. I can't sort anything out. I tend to jump around a lot."

"You do," Phyllis agreed.

"All the same, I still keep thinking about Little John and Sara. There is something I have to do about them. They were so happy or so Moon Rose told me. They were like a world I could never have."

"Did you ever see the child?"

"No. I wanted to but I felt I would be intruding. I called Moon Rose when I wanted to know how they were doing. She called me when he got into any trouble."

Phyllis snorted. "You were afraid of them."

"I don't think so," Shirley's voice trailed off. Perhaps Phyllis is right, she thought.

"They were your own personal soap opera," Phyllis said. "You kept away so you would not have to feel. You stayed apart."

"But safest he who stands aloof."

"But Milton you are not."

"Moon Rose said Sara was always quoting poetry. That was another way to stand aloof."

"Can you find out where Sara is now? Do you think she's still in Montreal?"

"I suppose I could find her. But he's not my case any more. She never was."

"But you've been obsessing about this thing for a while."

"I know – I know."

"Was he real? Or was he Memorex?"

"He was about being young. About music when nobody else could sing."

"And now?"

"Now it seems something is drying up. I need to know what's happening to them."

They sipped champagne.

"Maybe we'll see a whale tomorrow," Phyllis said.

"Maybe," Shirley replied, looking at a black and white sea, black and white sky and gray mounds of sand where faint shapes moved in the low-lying mist.

She thought again about Sara and Little John.

"I wonder if he loved her," she said.

"Have you ever loved a man?" Phyllis asked.

"They are tough to love, according to my clients anyway."

The mist thickened.

"Anyhow, I think I'd have to be loved first," Shirley went on. "And I'm not the type men usually love. I've known that all along. That's why I became a lawyer rather than getting married and becoming a housewife."

Phyllis laughed. "I think if loving a man makes you into housewife, I'd rather not. That's why my men flee so fast."

"Oh, you know that love can be more than that. It's just not something I know much about. I do think Sara loved John very much. I'm not sure about him."

"He left her."

"That's the other side of love. The dying ember. She had a tough time. It must be terrible to love someone so much that your life is not your own and then to be left alone to put it back together when he leaves you."

"Why did he leave her?"

"Perhaps he did not love her after all; perhaps he could not settle in one spot. He had no sense of time anyway. He had kept moving on, since he was a child. They kept moving him on until he couldn't stop."

"Like you?"

"Like me?" Shirley stared at her friend. "I am the essence of predictability. I never move on. I am always on time and my clients think I am a rock."

"You just seem that way," Phyllis told her. "You're like the sea out there beyond the breakers. You look solid and stable. The sea looks like flat black steel. It actually is constantly moving and has a whole world underneath it. You are moving on all the time. You just haven't noticed."

"You never settled down either. At least, not in the traditional way."

"I haven't figured men out. I think they are happy. I think we are happy. Then they go."

"Do you know why?"

"Oh, we stay friends. Perhaps I spent too much time thinking and reading when I was younger and I never learned the tricks."

"The tricks?"

"The tricks to keep men with you, to make them want to share your life."

"I don't think they do."

"What?"

"Want to share a life. Most of the divorces I handle are more about control than sharing. Neither the man nor the woman want to share anything unconditionally, especially what they feel. They want to control the other person. As long as the other person agrees to the control, they call it sharing. When the other person stops being controlled, the marriage is over."

"Both men and women?"

"Both. They just try to control in different ways. You should hear how ridiculous that becomes and sometimes it's tragic; like when they fight over a child. Sometimes I think there is no love anywhere, just different kinds of control – some easier to handle than the others."

"That's pretty bleak."

"I know. I don't think it was always this way."

"When was it different?"

"When romance was believed in, not viewed as a way to be entertained or a way to sell underwear. Perhaps when people really believed in love, honor and discretion, and really felt those things to be true – the way to be."

"Long ago and far away?"

"These days, I wonder if the only real emotions left are anger and a lust for power or control," Shirley murmured.

"You need to do something to prove yourself wrong." Phyllis told her.

"What might that be?"

"You need to find those two romantics. Perhaps you can help them."

"Who says they want or need my help?"

"That's the point. You need to feel you need to help them, whether you can or not. Then it won't matter. Perhaps you can't control anything. But you can let yourself feel, feel something that has no definition."

"Like a sound?"

"Or a poem before it grows words."

Shirley snorted. Sometimes Phyllis was a little too pedantic.

"I am a rock!" Shirley sang. "You are the o-ocean!"

The next morning, they walked between the storm-tossed logs half-buried by sand. Massive boulders ringed the bay. The surf formed, rolled and reshaped itself into breakers that smacked against the gritty sand, grinding small stones into perfect balls.

Perhaps that's why the sound is so peaceful, Shirley thought – edges grinding down so things can roll and go on without stopping, with no cutting edges.

Thousands of years ago, the First People landed their canoes here, and began to build a civilization. They knew that each human has many souls, has many faces. The raven was the sun, was a small boy, was a mask to dance with. Perhaps that's why this wild wind comforts me, why it smooths the jagged edges of my spirit. Spirit faces live here among the craggy, satin drift logs and soft blowing hemlocks.

Look at those!" Phyllis cried from atop an eight-foot log.

"What are they?"

"They're cormorants, I think they were sacred to the Haida. They are strange birds."

Two of the birds separated from the flock and chased each other against the misted sky. They dove through a tall breaker, disappearing into the foam for a second, then emerging on the other side.

"Those are fine," Phyllis sighed.

"Those are fine," Shirley agreed. "I'm glad we did this."

"Are they mating?" .

"I don't know."

They found a seat on a log and looked at the sea. On the edge of the horizon, a red sail was a triangular pointer to a cottage cheese sky.

Shirley let the wind and the wave sounds beat through her. The taste of salt was on her lips.

"Will you go with me?" she asked.

"Where?"

"Down the coast to Abraham. I want to visit Aunt Audrey."

"I think you need to do this on your own," Phyllis said.
Shirley nodded. A seagull screamed.

Chapter Ten

Katy grinned at the cards clenched in her hands.

"Trump!" she cried.

Philip scowled. He placed his cards face down. His eyes flickered.

"You win," he drawled. "What now?"

"What now?" she rasped. "What now? How the hell should I know?"

"We have to do something. He's not going to last long," Philip said.

She glared malevolently up at the black-beamed ceiling.

"He's a stubborn old fart."

"Have you asked him to do it?"

She curled her fist and banged on the tabletop. The cards jumped and flew.

"Asked him? Asked him?"

Philip heaved his ponderous body out of the chair and waddled over to the hearth.

He looked gloomily at the photograph of a farm hung above the mantle. He did not see the red barn, the brown winding road and bright green trees. He saw his father in bed upstairs, attended by a nurse.

But despite Big John's bleached skin and hollowed eyes, despite his claw-like hands, despite his stinking, rattling breath – despite all of that, the old man clung to life.

He even clings to sanity, although he has no good reason to do that either – and worst of all, he clings to the old will, Philip brooded.

And there is absolutely no reason to do that. Why won't he write my so-called step-brother out of the will?

Now he still wants to see that bastard again. And I know that John is dead. He has to be dead. But where did he die? They can't tell me. I can't prove it. And even if they find out he's dead; there's the brat. I didn't know about her when I had them do it. I should have known. But now? What now? The old man has to disinherit him. That's what now.

Philip ground his teeth.

****

Philip remembered Katy's anger when the Seattle police officer called to tell them that Sara was in jail. Katy had answered the telephone. The officer explained that her daughter, Sara, had been arrested and that her grandchild, Lucy, was in protective custody. Would she come and get the child?

"A child!" Katy cried. "What child?"

A child, the officer told her, a little girl.

Katy and two lawyers from Rolled, Smythe and Right went to Seattle.

The lawyers checked Lucy's birth records and found out that Little John was the child's father. They could not find Little John.

Katy wanted Lucy to remain a ward of the court. She wanted nothing to do with her.

"That child's a freak!" Katy cried. "She's the product of incest!"

As sick as he was, Big John did not agree. He didn't like Philip and Katy irritated him. After all, Big John thought, Sara and his oldest son were not really brother and sister. Relationships between step-brothers and sisters had been common in the south, he remembered. At the same time, blood was blood, family was family.

Big John's lawyer made a deal with Sara. Sara would go away, start over. Lucy would get the very best of care somewhere else.

They would keep looking for Little John. Big John hoped his son would come home and straighten things out. He wanted to see him again.

****

Little John better be dead, Philip prayed. But there was still a problem with Sara and her kid. The old man upstairs had to fix that, had to disown them completely.

What could have happened? Little John just disappeared. He could still be alive somewhere, the lawyers said. We are looking for him, they told Philip. Philip did not believe they were looking hard enough. He knew there had to be a body somewhere but he couldn't tell them that.

You never know. He could turn up at any time, the lawyers said.

Philip leaned his head on the mantle and balled his hands.

This is NOT fair. I am the real son. I work hard. I run all the businesses. I've opened hotels and inns along the coast. The estate is worth millions.

There's money in the bank. Lots of it. I put it there. It should all be mine.

Developers are swarming up and down the Oregon coast like ants on cheese, he thought. Abraham will soon be jammed with resorts, developments, golf courses, time shares and condominiums. If I'm left to run things on my own, I'll be a billionaire, one of the richest men in the country.

But unless the old fart changes his will, that kid and her mother will inherit millions as soon as he dies. Even if "Little John" is dead. Sara and the kid will be able to control what happens to the business.

Philip felt tears pushing at his eyes.

God knows how many other drug-ridden bastards that guy spawned. God knows how many more kids Sara might have. The old man upstairs must change that will.

"Son of a bitch," Philip muttered.

****

Katy glared at her son's back.

Sometimes she wondered why this boy, this boy of the best blood, had turned out so soft and slimy. He reminded her of a frog.

"The doctor doesn't give the old man much time," she said.

Philip did not react.

Speak to me. Why do you never speak? Speak. What are you thinking of? I never know what you are thinking, Katy thought. She sensed darkness in her son.

"I don't believe that old man will ever die," Philip said petulantly.

"Your father!"

Philip turned and looked at his mother.

"My father."

Footsteps shuffled on the stair.

There was a knock on the door.

"Who?" Katy asked.

Audrey came in; her eyes were wide and crazed.

Like Katy, she had grown smaller with age but Audrey was more like a raisin, crinkled and tiny, still essentially sweet.

"I have to talk to you!" she cried.

Katy surveyed her with surprise.

"Why now?" Katy asked.

Audrey bustled into the room and folded herself briskly into a wicker chair facing the card table.

"Because we have to do something!"

"Something?"

"We have to find Little John. Get things right. This is all wrong."

Philip turned away from the mantle and stared warily at his aunt.

"What's wrong?" he asked.

"All of it!"

"It?"

"All. He needs to know his father is dying. He needs to know where his little girl has gone and where Sara is."

"He needs!" cried Philip. This was too much. "Needs!"

He stopped, dumbfounded by anger. His mouth gaped open and then snapped shut.

Katy cleared her throat.

"I don't think so," she said dryly.

"Why not?" Aunt Audrey's voice quavered.

"He's a drug addict and a wastrel. She's a whore. The child is an abomination. I want nothing to do with any of them."

"I know Big John does!"

"He is a dying old fool," Katy said.

"You say that! You're his wife!"

Katy shrugged and looked down at the cards lying flat on the table.

Audrey stood up, quivering with anger and sadness.

"When he dies, you'll have to acknowledge them."

"He still can change his will," Philip said hopefully.

Audrey hooted.

"He never will. I know him."

Katy looked at her sister-in-law.

"You may be right. But if they try to claim anything – anything. They are in for a fight. This estate belongs to Philip. He has worked it for years."

Audrey shook her head sadly.

"I came to see you because that lady lawyer came to see me," she said. Breath pushed the words out like bullets. "After all these years, she still cares about him and worries about him. I couldn't help her. I don't know where he is. I told her that. She went away. But I thought I'd let you know. I have always worried about Little John. But what with Gary being so sick, I didn't have time to do anything. But now my Gary is gone, I want to see John again. I want to find him, or at least, make sure his little girl is OK."

"No sense in bothering now. You should mind your own business. Stay away from the kid. She's fine where she is. Fine not knowing what she is," Katy said.

"He's a sweet boy. I remember him. I remember his music," Audrey said.

Philip snorted.

Audrey walked to the door. She turned again and looked at the quivering mass of a man and his dried-up sparrow of a mother.

"His music," she repeated and left the room.

****

A few weeks later, Big John Finchley shifted in his bed in an effort to sit up. The last leaf on the branch outside his room let go and sank to the mud below the window. The wind outside whistled in the edge of winter.

Katy leaned forward in the rocker. Reverend Tim Bosworth of the Methodist Church leaned forward. He waited for Big John to say something, to turn to him for something.

Big John's life was fastened to his body by tubes and bags hung from shiny metal stands. The nurse, knitting in the shadowed corner, made sure that he would not be free of the machinery until the right time. She did not know when that right time would be but she had seen many people die when she least expected it.

She was usually summoned to homes when the hospitals released patients rich enough to leave the planet from their own beds. The nurse knew their end times were near but she would keep the tubes flowing as long as the fluids were useful.

Big John pushed his arm up as if reaching for something.

"Where is he?" he croaked. The shadow of a small boy danced behind his lids on the edge of a bright, white place. The boy was calling to him.

"Where is he?"

Katy sprang up. "Where's who?" she shouted, as if her voice could reach the place where Big John was headed. "The lawyer? He's downstairs. I'll get him."

Big John's eyes snapped open and shone with clear comprehension. Big John was, for that moment, back solidly in the land of the living.

He glared at her. Pure dislike pushed from his stare.

"Lawyer! Fuck Lawyer! I want my son!"

Katy sighed.

"Philip had to go to Seattle. He'll be back tonight."

Big John's eyes closed.

"Not him, not that pig," he muttered. "I want to see John."

"He don't care," Katy said. "You know we contacted him, and he said he was never coming home. He don't care if you live or die."

Katy didn't want to lie in front of the preacher but she had convinced herself that if they actually contacted Little John, he would say something like that. She looked over at the Reverend Bosworth but his fingertips were touching and his eyes were closed as if he were praying.

Big John's eyes snapped open again.

"You said that lawyer is downstairs? Get him here!"

Hope and gratitude filled Katy's mind as she rushed down the stairs to the parlor where Harold Sadd sat in the leather recliner, reading *The New York Times*.

Harold represented Miller, Slimmer and Sadd, the Seattle law firm that currently represented the Finchleys. Before he became ill, Big John had read a newspaper article about how Benjamin Rolled of Rolled, Smythe and Right had been charged and imprisoned for child abuse.

"That bunch will not represent MY family!" Big John said and transferred all his business to a law firm recommended by one of his board members.

Katy had summoned Sadd to Abraham to be on hand in case her husband decided to change his will before he died. She hoped it would be soon because she knew Sadd collected an hourly fee, in addition to a large retainer, and had no problem making hundreds of dollars reading a newspaper as he waited.

"He wants you!" Katy cried. "He wants YOU!"

Sadd folded up the paper and struggled to his feet. Recliners are much easier to get into than out of, he thought. He followed Katy to Big John's deathbed.

"Ah the vulture," Big John croaked.

Harold Sadd allowed himself to smile.

"I want to change my will," Big John whispered.

Big John waited for Sadd to take out a notepad and pen. "Come closer."

Sadd winced. He hated sickness and death and the thought of Big John breathing on him filled him with disgust. He bent cautiously over the bed. Big John's whisper was clear as a bell.

"I'm not changing the part about Philip running and owning the timber business. That's his. I want to change the part about the savings, stocks and real estate. I want my oldest son, John, to get half of that. The other forty percent is to go to my step-daughter

Sara. My wife gets the house and ten percent. If John dies, or, God help me, if he is already dead – his share goes to Sara and any children he might have had, split evenly. Family is family."

Sadd pursed his lips.

"In the will you already signed, your son John, and his children, would inherit ten percent of your estate outside the timber business. Your step-daughter, Sara, would get the other ten percent. Your wife, Katy, and your son, Philip, would get the remaining eighty percent. Are you sure you want to change that? Your son, Philip said you wanted to change the will so that he would get one hundred percent of the savings, stocks and real estate."

Big John closed his eyes.

"He is full of shit. Make the changes I want now." he gasped.

"If we cannot find your oldest son, who will be your executor?" Sadd asked.

"You guys, as before," Big John said.

Katy let out a small shriek and covered her mouth. She wanted to scream loudly, to shout, to protest. Sadd had told her that there was nothing anybody could do if the old man added to or changed the will while he was of sound mind. Like Philip, she had wanted a completely different set of changes.

Perhaps his mind is not sound? She looked at the Reverend and at the nurse in the corner. Perhaps they could help later.

Sadd nodded and said, "I'll be back tomorrow with something for your signature."

The next morning, gray rain drifted sideways against the house. Big John was still alive but something shapeless waited in the shadows.

Katy, the nurse and Reverend Bosworth were in the room. Nobody moved or spoke when Sadd came in and approached the bed. He held a sheet of paper on a clipboard.

"Can you sign?" he asked the still figure.

Big John opened his eyes and nodded. The hand that made the signature shook a little but it knew what it was doing.

Sadd turned to the watchers.

"I need two witnesses."

The nurse moved forward and signed. The Revered Bosworth stopped praying long enough to sign. Sadd looked at Katy. She remained motionless.

Sadd left the room.

A gust of wind breathed a long, low sound, as if it marked the time that Big John stopped leaving tracks. The nurse took his pulse and lifted his eyelids. She began to remove the tubes from his arms and from his nose. She dictated the time into a tape recorder.

****

"And now? What now?" Katy cried that evening.

Big John had been officially pronounced dead and Sadd was packing his briefcase. Audrey was back in the house to help prepare for the funeral. Katy had called her because she said she was to upset to handle the job herself.

"Don't worry. I'll arrange for the food for the reception and the Reverend Bosworth will speak at the service," Audrey said.

Katy gave her a withering look and looked accusingly at Sadd.

"Not that! What about the estate? The savings accounts?"

Katy knew that Big John had several million dollars in his savings accounts for quick transfer to the checking accounts as he needed. His investments also were worth several million.

"When can we access our share?"

"Not for a while," Sadd told her. "We have to find out if that oldest son is alive or dead and contact any of his children. In the meanwhile the will is in probate. Things can go on as before until the estate is settled.

"We will determine the value of the investments and manage them for you. As you know, your husband named my firm as executor of the estate. We must keep his best interests in mind."

"What about my interests! Mine and Philip's!"

The lawyer remained silent.

"What now?" Katy asked again.

"We have to find the other son."

"If he's dead? If he's gone?"

"If that is proved, we find his children."

"If you can't find him?"

"That part of the estate remains in probate until he is found."

"If he is dead but we don't know how many other children he has?"

"We have to prove he is dead and then search for other heirs. We can do that through legal postings in newspapers and, although it is unlikely there will be a response, it has to be done and it will take time."

"The court decides? What my husband didn't know what he was doing when he changed the will? All those pills. He was half-dead! Out of his mind!"

"You'll have to prove that. Those claims can take years."

"I don't care!" Katy cried. "I'm ready."

"That's your right."

"And what about the child we do know about?"

"I think we should tell her what has happened and let her mother make contact with her."

"No! My contract with your firm specifies your discretion! The revelation of a child born from incest in the Finchley family could destroy our reputation! Lower the value of the company stocks!"

"I doubt that," Sadd said.

Katy looked at him coldly. "If you break our agreement, I will find another bunch of lawyers to represent us and ask them to find a way we can stop paying for her support," she said.

"We won't break the agreement we made with you but once the court releases the funds, she will have to be told. In any case, the mother has the right to contact her daughter if she wishes," Sadd said coldly.

"She signed an agreement!"

"She can still break that agreement. She is no longer dependent on you for support. We should let her know the terms of the new will."

"She doesn't need to know anything until it actually happens," Katy said. "Let's wait until the court decides who gets what. Tell her anything now and you lose our business."

"At this point, we will do as you say," Sadd said, knowing he was stretching his ethics. However, Finchley Incorporated was an important client. He needed to think of a way to serve his client and the law. What a nasty woman, he thought, snapping his briefcase shut. I am glad to get out of here.

Audrey felt angry. Since Gary had died, she had not thought of a good reason to go on much longer herself. Now she did. Little John should not be denied his birthright. He and his child would be set for life. She would wait and watch and see what she could do.

"I am ready too," she said softly.

Meanwhile, there were things to cook and a burying to organize.

Chapter Eleven

Shirley maneuvered Griselda between the slow-moving cars, scooters and bicycles crowding steep, narrow streets to Nester Slimmer's home on Capitol Hill. It had been built before Seattle's wealthy moved across the lake. The area went to seed during the 1960s. Then the resident flower children blossomed into lawyers, doctors and social workers.

"I remember when Nester Slimmer was on the board of the *Seattle Moon*," Phyllis said. "His clients were always being sued for making various types of protest."

Phyllis and Shirley were going to an artistic happening hosted by Slimmer, and his wife, Jasmine. Phyllis' agent was Louise Stamplin. Louise also represented guitarist Cory Simpson, Jasmine's latest project. When Jasmine Slimmer entertained, she invited everybody's useful connections. Phyllis, as a poet, was a minor celebrity in her own right and Shirley was her guest.

"Those were the days," Shirley sighed.

"Wasn't that when you first started dealing with that musician, John?" Phyllis asked.

Shirley clenched her jaw.

"It was."

"It's too bad you never found him."

Shirley nodded and sighed again.

"His trail just dead-ended."

"That was odd."

"It's still odd," Shirley said. "I thought about him again today and made a couple of calls. You won't believe it. The Finchley estate's been in litigation for years. Our host helps it stay tangled since he is retained by the family and is paid handsomely each month to keep everything unsettled."

"Wasn't the family a client of your old Portland firm, Rolled, Smythe and Right? How come Slimmer?"

"Something pissed off the old man before he died, I guess. He transferred all his business to Miller, Slimmer and Sadd. Made no difference. It's still unsettled."

"What would settle it?"

"They need to prove whether Little John is dead or alive, and if he is dead, that he has only one child. At first, they were trying to prove the old man insane when he rewrote the will leaving half his estate to his oldest son. That idea, I believe, has been pretty much thrown out, although the younger son Philip keeps bringing it up. That one has become obsessed with the whole thing. If anybody is nuts, Philip is."

"The daughter – what was her name – still doesn't know what's going on?"

Shirley shook her head.

"They've decided to keep everything from Lucy until it's all settled. Her guardian is Larry Miller, one of our host's partners. He feels she too fragile or something. I asked him about that but he can't tell me why. Move it!"

Shirley honked at a woman with a wicker backpack strolling across a pedestrian walkway just slowly enough to make Shirley miss the light.

"Messy," Phyllis said.

"Annoying! Oh, you mean the Lucy situation. Yup."

****

Nester Slimmer had just graduated from law school when he bought the house. To keep the house maintained, he married Jasmine Saunders who was well supported by a large trust fund.

Jasmine befriended local artists, gave them donations and hosted receptions for them in her regularly redecorated living room.

There were no Slimmer children. The couple's relationship was peaceful but platonic. Their friends knew Slimmer preferred the beautiful young men who wandered around Volunteer Park across the road.

Shirley swore as she drove Griselda around the block for a second time. "It's impossible to park around here."

"Sometimes you can find something in a back alley. It's a good thing you're still driving this bug."

"No shit. That's why they're coming back in."

"I like yours better than the new models."

"This old girl is on her sixth engine. She'll outlast me. Here we are."

Shirley slipped Griselda into a barely big-enough spot between garbage cans. They climbed out and wandered up the alley. A light mist fell as they walked around to the front door.

Jasmine dashed through her foyer and flung her arms around Phyllis.

"Oh Hi!" Jasmine drawled. "I'm so glad you can make it! I love your work!!"

Phyllis stiffened and nodded.

"This is my friend, Shirley."

Jasmine smiled, said "Hello-pleased-to-meet-you," and evaporated into the living room on the other side of wide wooden doors.

Shirley hung up her coat.

"This could be grim," she told Phyllis.

"Oh, come on," Phyllis replied doubtfully. She kept her shawl wrapped tightly around herself.

The huge living room, filled with animated humans, was lined in cedar and weighted with antiques. An elaborate buffet of couscous, shellfish, sushi, salads and baked goods covered a long table against the wall.

Shirley lumbered into the throng behind her friend.

God, I hate these things, she thought. I don't understand why Phyllis likes to flutter among these would-be artists. I guess she likes to match wits. Although, in this bunch, there does not appear to be much of a match. There rarely is.

Shirley found the food and stuffed a tiny quiche into her mouth.

"Well, well, Shirley," Slimmer murmured from beside her elbow. She started and looked down at the somewhat-smiling attorney. He looks like a crow, she thought.

"Hi," she said with her mouth full, recalling her conversation with Felix Oswood. She hoped Slimmer found her equally repulsive.

"Glad you could come," he said, seemingly undeterred.

"How's business?" he asked.

She swallowed and toothed back at him.

"There is no shortage of deewees, divorces or delinquents."

He expanded his mouth even further.

Now he looks like a Haida totem pole, Shirley decided. A Haida crow.

"How's your business?" she asked, feeling once again the surge of happiness she felt every time she remembered that her days of servitude at Rolled, Smythe and Right were over.

What a bunch they all are, she thought. They bleed their clients to the bone. Perhaps he's more of a vulture than a crow. But he's too small. Both birds eat road kill.

"Oh, fine," he said.

"Any progress in the Finchley case?"

He placed a forefinger along his nose and glanced at her sideways.

"We keep going. We keep going."

I bet you do, Shirley thought.

Remembering Little John and his music saddened her so she reached for another quiche.

At the other end of the room, Jasmine stepped up onto a small platform set up in the bay window. Her long black hair fell down over one eye so she grabbed it with ring-weighted fingers and pulled it tightly to one side.

The room's buzz subsided as her flat voice rose.

"Hey guys," she droned and grinned.

Why does she call everybody guys? Shirley wondered.

"I have someone I want you all to meet and to listen to. Please welcome Cory Simpson," Jasmine said, never letting her mouth close over her perfect teeth.

The sky outside the window darkened. Spider plants in the violet light hung head down in the shadowed room. Slimmer closed his stretched lips and sidled to a couch beside the platform.

Shirley, her mouth dried by quiche crumbs, backed away from the table and looked around for Phyllis. Her friend was watching the platform with her head cocked on one side, looking like an inquisitive sparrow.

Jasmine beckoned to a tall, white-haired man carrying a guitar. He moved forward as the audience parted for his progress.

A Moses in a sea of Philistines. The sixties were good to this guy, Shirley thought. She glanced at Phyllis.

Phyllis' eyes twinkled back in the shared observation. Their minds met and giggled.

Cory Simpson's hair was caught in a thick braid that fell to his waist. A row of rings pierced his right eyebrow. Tattoos encircled his wiry arms. When he faced the audience, his eyes were half hidden by small wire glasses caught on the end of a long nose that tapered up just enough at its point to hold the spectacles.

When he began to play, Shirley gasped.

She knew, knew to her bones, who first played those sounds and when. These are the same notes, almost with the same cadence, not quite as intense, not quite as demanding, she thought.

But there, there it is – the slide harmonics, the grating rhythms, the sound she remembered from the smoky room with the hanging beads – the Aggervawn, where Little John grabbed a piece of her mind and never gave it back. She recognized the guitar. It had to be his.

Cory added words to the music. Later, Shirley could not remember what they were. Her memories of Moon Rose, swinging beads and Little John's marching fingers overpowered her.

I must speak to this man. He must have known Little John, known what happened to him, know where he's gone. He must know that.

The sound was there again. Once again, it brought Tennyson's words to her mind: *One set slow bell would seem to toll, the remembrance of the sweetest soul...*

After the tones had faded and last harmonic sounded from the Gibson's strings, the room rattled with applause.

Jasmine smiled proudly. It was clear she had found herself a winner.

The sounds of the 1960s have gained new popularity these days, Shirley thought. That studded and tattooed Cory is positioned to be a retro hero in this town, although it usually waits until its musicians die before it makes them famous.

Suddenly, she knew Little John was dead and that Cory knew it too. Little John's spirit cried through Cory's fingers.

It was hard to wait through the encore, through the small talk, through the white wine and the clamor.

Phyllis wanted to leave the party as soon as he finished playing but Shirley had to stay until she could talk to Cory.

Finally, Cory left the crowd and headed for the room where he could put down his guitar and sit down. He told the new-age groopies who hung on his lanky frame that he would be right back.

Shirley pushed her way past them, followed Cory and shadowed him as he bent to lay down the guitar on the bed. He sat beside it. She watched as he fumbled in his pocket for the joint he had saved. He could no longer take the babble and the brittle air without a drag of the mellow green.

Shirley loomed large and filled the room.

Cory looked up at her. His eyes were startled behind his glasses.

"What happened to Barefoot John?" Shirley demanded. "Why are you playing his music? Isn't that his guitar?"

"Wow," he breathed.

"Well?"

"Wow," he said again, shaking his head. He lit the end of his joint with a pink plastic lighter held in a shaking hand and inhaled deeply.

Shirley waited.

"It's been a long time," he exhaled.

"How long?"

He frowned and looked up at her impatient face. Something else about her, something beyond that, made him say:

"Sit down. Relax." He inhaled and held his breath as he waved his hand at a chair near the bed. She sat. The chair creaked.

"You want to know what happened to Barefoot John?" he asked as he breathed out.

She nodded.

"I haven't heard from him since he sent a chick to visit me long time ago," he said. "I didn't actually see him then either. Right? But one day this chick, this worn out chick, think she was a hooker, you

know? Anyhow, she comes to the house one day. I was doin' OK
back then. I was working construction, making good bucks
remodeling old houses in this town and I still was playin' music here
and there. When she arrived, I was on my way to do a gig at the
Bumbershoot festival. It was their opening day, a Friday."

"You played music with him before then?"

"Oh yeah. Couple of years before then. That was our scene then.
We had this rock jug band, right? Called Acid Flash. We were pretty
cool. Jug band music, blues and shit."

"What happened to the band?

"Well, we were in Portland, groovin'. But you know, things
changed," Cory's voice floated off.

"What changed?" Shirley tried to mask her impatience.

He smiled sadly.

"Well, I was not the best musician in the band. They were always
telling me I was screwing up. Then I met Beverly and she pretty
much straightened me out. The others, Barefoot and Pierce, they
were getting into heavier drugs than I liked and she made me
choose."

"You chose her."

He nodded.

"It was a good choice. We got married, had Cheryl. That's my
daughter and we were happy for a long time."

He paused and inhaled again.

"Then, you know. Things change. Now I'm divorced and trying
to get back into the music scene," he exhaled.

"And Barefoot John?" Shirley prompted so that he wouldn't stray
from the topic at hand and start talking about himself.

"Barefoot John. Yeah." He frowned, recollecting with effort.
"Well, after I married Beverly we moved in with my Mom; she was
sick and needed my help. I started work and lost track of the band.
Then one day, out of the blue, like I said, this chick shows up and

tells me John's down in some old building on the waterfront. Says he's real sick, tells me he's in a pad we used to party in, long time ago, you know? Then she splits before I get more information. Like she just runs away."

"You found him?"

Cory shook his head.

"Nah. I couldn't get there until the next day. I had to play, like I said. Then it was late, getting dark. I went to look for him in the morning. After all he'd been my man, right? My friend, you know? Anyhow, when I got there, he was gone. I wandered around the place a little. It was, like, a real drag. The building was a dump. Rat shit everywhere. But I found his guitar and his backpack."

"But not him?"

Cory shook his head.

"No sign of him at all ?" Shirley asked.

Cory shook his head.

"I waited there for him for a while. Then I figured he might be going to my house, where he'd sent the chick. Maybe he'd felt better enough to get there or something. Anyway, he had sent her to me. I knew he wouldn't want me to leave his shit there and I couldn't wait for him forever. I figured he'd know to come to my house if he got back to the place and his stuff was gone."

"You're playing his guitar."

Cory nodded.

"You sound so much like him," Shirley said.

Cory chuckled.

"That would piss him off. He always said I played like shit."

"Do you still have the backpack?" Shirley asked.

Cory nodded.

"After a while, when I didn't hear from him, I thought his backpack might would have an address or something in it. All it had was some song lyrics, a lot of tapes – you know – those old reel-to-reel types. And there was this letter with no address, to somebody called Lucy. It sounded like his kid."

Shirley felt her heart thud.

"You have that letter still?"

He nodded.

Shirley looked at Cory in disbelief.

"Nobody tracked you down? Nobody came to you and asked about him? I know his family and his lawyers have been trying to find out what happened to him for years."

"No," he said. "But then I didn't use the name Simpson when I was with Acid Flash. I didn't want the draft board to find me. Nobody would have ratted me out back then and a lot of years have passed since then."

"Can you show me that letter?"

"You figure he's dead."

She nodded.

Cory looked sadly at the guitar.

"Yeah. He's gotta be. He would have shown up by now."

"Can you remember what year that was?"

Cory grinned.

"I was thinking about that today. They've asked me to play at the Bumbershoot festival again, that Seattle Center gig has been around for twenty-eight years. I kind of got a kick out of that because I wondered if they would let me play twenty-eight songs."

"Excuse me?"

"Well, I remembered the year I picked up Barefoot's stuff – it was their eighth festival. I played eight songs, one for each year."

Phyllis gasped.

"And you played on the first Friday of that Labor Day weekend?"

Cory nodded.

"That would be in 1978."

"Yup."

"You picked up Little John's stuff the next day, which would have been the Saturday of the Labor Day weekend in 1978."

"Seems right."

Chapter Twelve

In downtown Seattle, rain pushed newspapers and cigarette butts into gutters, swirled in puddles and rushed down drains to underground ghosts and cobblestones. It flowed into the flat and black saltwater Sound without surf or waves.

A lonely horse lounged against the curb, leaning on the traces of its buggy. It lowered its blinkered head against the wet.

Just as low was the helmeted head of the bicycle courier, pedaling through gritty streams, bare legs blue in the driving rain, the body of a child but with the sunken eyes and drawn face of an old man. He pedaled over cobblestones to the courthouse, up against the gray, pushing gravity away with each stroke as water ran down his shins. The documents he carried would change lives and end others.

He rode past headlights cutting through the misted noon. Around him, cars inched behind each other, like pavement slugs. He passed eaves and overpasses sheltering the bearded, the bald, the white-haired, the sick and the young who never looked up at the white squares of light stacked around them in cement towers.

He rode past offices where slick and young professionals clicked fingers against plastic; meditated upon glowing cursors and closed their ears to the sounds around them.

He rode past bars squeezed in narrow corridors between the buildings near the courthouse. There, petitioner and pimp, bondsman, councilor, worker and workless pondered their problems in the foam of cheap, micro, dark and light liquids.

In the courthouse, judges huddled under black cloaks, bleak-eyed crows on the fences of justice. They were isolated in chambers, blocked from the streets and the ranks of the resigned huddled in the waiting rooms around them.

The courier pushed his bicycle up the steps, went inside and handed the envelope to the clerk in Courtroom No. 1.

Audrey, with pleated plastic on her head, waited in the back of the courtroom, sorting the shiny agates she pulled from a large shopping bag. Each time another lawyer began to speak, her head jerked upright and her body froze. When she realized they were saying nothing new, her head went back down and she continued her work. Nobody wondered what she was doing there because nobody cared. She had been in the courtroom every morning for months, leaving as soon as she heard the date of the next continuance.

That morning she had been listening for more than an hour. Then the door behind her opened and a courier scurried up the aisle and handed an envelope to the clerk. The clerk handed it to one of the lawyers. The lawyer stopped drawing a naked woman on his notepad and opened the envelope. He read its contents and handed the papers to the lawyer beside him who also read the words and stood up.

"Approach your honor?"

The judge nodded. The lawyers and the judge murmured something in low voices. Audrey couldn't understand what they were saying but she noticed the papers were read, reread and then handed to the court clerk who gave them a number and filed them away.

The judge said the session would be continued in another month, so attorneys could evaluate the new information. He adjourned the proceeding.

Audrey left the courtroom.

She saw the lawyers grinning at each other as they walked past her. They were heading across the street for beer.

"How long we been at this?" mused one.

"It's been a while," replied another. "It was with Rolled, Smythe and Right before, but Rolled – well – you know about Rolled."

"The child?" wondered the third.

"Still in in the dark," replied the third. "For now."

"What now? Shouldn't she know?"

"We need to make sure he's dead."

"Isn't he?"

"We need to make sure. That letter isn't proof of anything. He could have written it and moved on."

"That could take a while."

"Hopefully."

That conversation ended; the elevator arrived.

Meanwhile, Audrey grabbed her bags and walked slowly toward the stairs. She didn't like elevators and she didn't like lawyers.

"Audrey? Audrey Smith?"

Audrey squinted at the large woman who blocked her passage.

"Hi, " she said, after she recognized the speaker.

"The lawyers left already," she said.

"I'm not here as a lawyer," Shirley replied.

"Why then?"

"Maybe I'm kind of his friend."

"He didn't have so many" Audrey sighed

"What are you going to do now?" Shirley asked.

"I will come back in a month. You never know."

"We have to prove he died," Shirley said.

Audrey looked up at her.

"Can you help?"

"I think so."

****

"Why are you doing this?" Phyllis asked Shirley.

"You found the letter. You gave it to the lawyers. You told them the date. Why can't you let it go?"

Shirley looked through the plate glass picture window at the cement spires marching to the waterfront.

"They aren't doing a thing about it," she said. "They say that the letter just proves he was alive back then and that he had a daughter called Lucy. It doesn't prove he's dead now."

Phyllis rolled her eyes.

"What will finish it for you? You have been thinking about this case since you first heard the kid play years ago. You even kept copies of his file when you left that law firm, which you were not supposed to do. Since that damn party, you've been obsessing on it. This is not good for you."

Shirley sighed. Sometimes Phyllis was too new age, too pop-psych.

"I want to know what happened to him. His Aunt Audrey has been hanging around the court for years. His kid needs to know what happened to him. In that letter, he said he loved her. It was as if he knew he was dying when he wrote it."

"Why don't the lawyers check it out? I don't get it."

Outside the apartment's window, a seagull caught the wind and flew backward.

"They've been living on this litigation for years."

"I'm surprised the estate hasn't gone broke."

Shirley barked a laugh.

"The lawyers manage it well. They have made sure the estate remains prosperous and keeps them in the style to which they have become accustomed."

"So what will finish it?" Phyllis repeated.

"Proof he's dead. Then, by law, the child and the mother will inherit their share and everything will come out in the open."

"That's good? Perhaps the kid is better off not knowing her mother abandoned her."

"She probably thinks that already."

****

Shirley drove Griselda down the hill to the old section of Seattle's waterfront between Pike Market and the ferry terminal where Cory had found Little John's backpack and guitar.

She wanted to make sure that Cory's memory of the address had been correct. The intersection still existed but the old buildings had been torn down and gleaming condominiums were stacked along the block.

If he had been sick in that old building, somebody might have called an ambulance, she thought. They would have taken him to Soundview Hospital. Even back then it was the death house for the unwanted and the unknown.

She gasped. She knew what to do. They take fingerprints when people die at Soundview. Little John's fingerprints were taken when he was arrested during a demonstration. That's the answer, she thought. That's it.

She drove back to her office, checked Little John's file and made an appointment to see the medical examiner at the hospital the next morning.

****

He was a gentle soft-spoken man, somewhere in his mid-fifties.

"We try everything we can to identify them," he told her. "But there is little we can do when the body has no identification. When we can't find anyone to claim it, it goes to the crematorium. We keep the death certificates and fingerprints on file.

"What date did you say your client was last seen?"

Shirley told him.

"We could never figure out what happened to him," she said. "His aunt has asked me to investigate. I was given the first clue just recently when I ran into an old friend of his who picked up his belongings where he had been seen last, on this date and at that address."

The examiner left Shirley in his office while he disappeared into the file room.

If there are ghosts, they must fill this place, Shirley thought.

And their sun does never shine, and their fields are bleak and bare, and their ways are fill'd with thorns. It is eternal winter there...

The examiner returned.

"We only had one pick-up at that address," he said. "No identification, a young man who died the same evening."

"What was wrong with him?

He looked down at the death certificate and the report in his hands.

"He had used cocaine. But that's not what killed him. He was poisoned. They found the drug in his system, all right, but they also found arsenic. Could have been rat poison. It seems it took him a couple of days to die."

"He was poisoned?"

"Looks like. Of course we can't find out more now."

"Did he eat rat poison in that building?" Shirley asked.

The examiner shook his head.

"The poison and the cocaine were ingested at the same time. He probably thought he had overdosed. You said he had friends here. Maybe he came home to die or to get better. Wild dogs do that you know."

"Excuse me?" Shirley blinked. What had wild dogs to do with anything?

The medical examiner sighed.

"People out there. These people."

He waved his hand at the file room behind him.

"They learn to live on the streets and most of the time they know where they want to die. In the woods, wild dogs do the same."

His tone was whimsical, Shirley realized he had thought about it a great deal. He was guardian of the victims of a world where fog was their shroud. Rain washed papers and lives into the sleek salty sea and people went to sleep forever on wooden benches.

... and parents their lost children mourn while their ashes lie in unknown urn...

Wild dogs and a barefoot boy, dying where they chose to dream.

"Yes," she said.

"You still have the fingerprints?" she asked.

"We have the prints, the report and the ashes. When it's a suspected homicide we keep the ashes. Evidence. You know."

"I think this is the proof I need," Shirley said. "In 1966, my client was arrested during a protest. Seattle police might have his fingerprints on file. If those prints match the ones in your file, the family can reclaim the ashes."

"Do you know the exact date of that charge?"

Shirley told him.

"Let me check the old police records," the medical examiner said. "If there's a match. I will find it. I'll call you. I'll let you know."

He smiled.

Shirley saw he was relieved to find the family of one of his charges and send one of his sad shades home

Shirley went home, walked out to her balcony and looked down at the glittering city. Washed with recent rain, ebony streets gleamed with jewels.

Down there, she thought. Down there, under that lovely and glowing surface, wandering souls wait for their passage; dying manatees in a polluted swamp.

Chapter Thirteen

Sara drove her blue BMW up the rain-slicked drive to the white brick mansion she now called home.

For years, my days have felt like this mist, she thought. There are no real boundaries between times, just different settings, different faces scowling at me, smiling at me, walking beside me. But there is nobody there, shape without form, shade without color, paralyzed force, gesture without motion.

She ordered words in her mind, another poem.

The rain has soaked my soul, stirring dull roots, and rain turns grass to emeralds.

She sighed.

That morning, her tweed-armed literature instructor, rather than illuminating her mind, had sent it sailing off to Mexico. She began the daydream when he said all Victorian poetry was written by writers who were sexually frustrated. He said the lines on the pages meant nothing as they were written. They could only be understood through reading other writings by other writers, who themselves, required interpretation.

Why did I still start taking English classes again after all this time? Sara wondered. What will I do with a Master's degree if I get one? That instructor will be reincarnated as a footnote. It's time for another trip to Puerto Vallarta. Robert won't mind. He never does. Sun will be good; the beach will be good. I have to get out of this gray.

Mexico, here I come. I need some sun. Robert should be home from the hospital by now. I can tell him I'm going.

The Porsche parked between the stone columns beside Robert's Mercedes was not a welcome sight.

Damn. Nester Slimmer is here. I hate the sight of him. He makes me feel sick and ruined. He knows about me. He says nothing. He can say nothing. But he knows. It is dark here. A storm is coming.

Sara shuddered, preparing herself for the way Slimmer's eyes slithered over her. She opened the carved cedar door to the main hall and walked into the coatroom to hang up her wet jacket. She listened to rain drumming on eaves and gutters.

Water dripped from the sleeves of Robert's London Fog raincoat and from Slimmer's brown leather car coat. They haven't been here long, she realized.

Sara looked at the three jackets and wondered why coats without people inside them were much more interesting than coats draped on ordinary human backs. The three garments in a row seemed sad, like a damp family at a train station. Sara stared at them for a while, at the water pooling on the floor and at the black umbrella leaking darkly in the corner. She smelled the damp, warm air of wet. She wished she could avoid facing the low murmur of voices coming from the library, avoid hearing what they were saying.

She walked slowly down the dark hall to the dark door and into the room where light was muted by the gloom outside the window and yellowed by the flicker in the huge fireplace.

Anywhere else that fire would be cozy, Sara mused. Here, overpowered by this expanse of gleaming wood floor, gold-framed mirrors and brass fixtures, it was not cozy but lonely as a campfire on a treeless field.

Slimmer and Robert were at the desk, Robert in the captain's chair. Slimmer sat backwards on a cane-back chair.

Robert looked a little grayer than usual and more tired. As she entered, his eyes flickered like a candle in a gust of wind. Slimmer looked sideways at her, his eyes expressionless and his lips pursed.

"Good afternoon, Mrs. Bradley," Slimmer said.

Sara kept her face opaque and nodded in his direction.

"Hello Darling. How was your day?" Robert said.

He is always so careful with me, Sara thought, as if I were made of china. So goes this world I am in.

She yawned, covered her mouth with one hand and, with her head tilted so her hair shrouded half of her face, wandered to the recliner nearest the fireplace. She settled into it and leaned forward.

"OK," she said. "What's up?"

Her tone was marginally interested.

"Oh, well –" Robert breathed.

He looks frightened, almost terrified, she thought as she lowered her eyes.

Slimmer anchored his stare on her.

She did not look at him. Her hair felt like a shield. Against what? Something in the air.

"It depends." Slimmer said.

He knew what depended upon what. He knew that so much depended on him that it was only fair that he could not be depended upon at all. He was only as dependable as he needed to be.

"It depends." Slimmer said again.

"Depends?" Sara murmured blandly, leaning back. She closed her eyes.

"Nester has been catching me up with your family's case." Robert said

Sara lay back in silence. She seemed to be sleeping. The men waited.

She lifted her head, opened her eyes and mouth.

"We can never catch up," she said.

Robert frowned slightly as if she had broken a carefully installed taboo.

Slimmer's lips twitched with amusement or scorn.

"We try," the lawyer said.

"Much good that does," Sara said.

She noted the flush rising to the attorney's cheeks.

Now Robert looked away. Sara felt his fear and wondered why she felt like crying.

"There is something new," Slimmer said.

"Something new?" she repeated.

"It is probably nothing," Slimmer murmured.

Oh, it is something. We all know it is something, she thought. The room was closing in.

Now Slimmer was smiling but his smile was shaped like a snarl. He selected a piece of paper from the pile on the desk and smoothed it out.

"Sara, I think you will be interested in this," he said. "One of my wife's clients had it all these years. Here."

He jabbed at a name at the bottom of the paper.

Sara unfurled herself from the recliner and stood up. She approached Slimmer warily as if he had a contagious disease. She leaned over the desk and studied the sheet.

She bent closer.

"He – Who wrote this?" she gasped.

She recovered herself. She felt blood leaving her face,

"That handwriting is just terrible," she muttered. "Who could ever read it?"

She looked over at Robert. His eyes were dark and sad.

Had he known all along? Did he know now? Now what?

Slimmer looked at her with locked eyes.

"Why, the person who wrote it and people who knew him," the lawyer said.

"Whatever," Sara shrugged. She turned to Robert.

"I'm going upstairs. I have some reading to do."

Robert nodded warily. His eyes were questions.

He wants to know what I'm thinking. I don't know what I am thinking. I am drowning.

"I'll see you later," Robert said.

Sara stood up in one fluid movement. Her face was as calm as the porcelain shepherdess on the mantel. She walked from the library, up the curving stairs to her room where she curled up in the bay window. Unblinking, she stared at the damp wetness of the bright green rolling lawn. Tears spilled down her chin and onto her hair.

She leaned her head against the cold glass.

I am drowning. He's come for me and I will drown in his memory. And she? Does she remember me? Does she hate me?

The rain seemed to pause; the agony faded into dark pain. It was time to turn back, to go back to the room wrapped in the quiet of death, the silence of the waiting phantom.

Sara knew what had to be done, knew what she had to do but could not face it, not just that second. She needed to see something first, feel something else. She wandered down the stairs and walked outside where the fog curled up from the lake, wrapped around the tulip tree and flowed over the damp grass. She leaned over the porch railing and looked across the rippling black water at the towers across the way, at a city grown so jagged so quickly. There were shadows in the mist and muffled drums in the lapping waves.

She went back inside and entered the study.

Slimmer was still backwards on the cane-back chair. Robert was still in the captain's chair, turning over papers, as if somewhere in that pile there was something he needed, perhaps an ending.

Slimmer muttered something she could not hear as he poked at the single sheet of hand-written paper. It was the one item that would settle the estate and answer the questions and was the one thing that should be considered – must be considered. It was time for that now. He was trying to explain what it meant to his client's husband. He knew the information was not welcome and had never been welcome.

Robert's eyes shifted away from the papers, to the wall, to the floor, anywhere but to the letter. He did not want any more information. He did not want to discuss it further. The mist that shrouded the past had been a good thing, a safe thing.

Robert murmured "Right," and looked away.

Slimmer realized again he had not been listened to. Slimmer started to repeat himself. There were things to consider. These considerations were significant.

Sara drifted into the room like a tendril of fog. Her face was opaque.

Robert looked up, saw her, caught his breath and looked down. Had his lovely crystal woman shattered? There was a dark sense of earth in her walk, as if gravity were dragging her feet into the ground.

As Sara walked toward him she felt that the fog outside had entered her and permeated her brain. Everything was vague and misty and slipping away, out of her control. As it went, it tore open a memory that pulled at her throat and filled her eyes with tears.

Surely not, she thought. I have no tears left.

Robert's eyes also were damp and dark with pain.

Was this still his Sara? he wondered. Something glittered on the high and perfect cheekbone and something made her perfect mouth tremble slightly.

Slimmer looked at the pair of them with satisfaction. His hooded eyes gleamed.

"It is clear what the young man wanted," Slimmer said.

"Clear!" Sara cried. "How clear!"

Robert started and stared.

"There was only one child," Slimmer whispered.

"Right," Robert murmured. "A child."

Sara's hands twisted and turned upon themselves. She could not look at her husband.

He knows.

What now?

She saw behind him her mother's dark shadow, clawed fingers reaching for her. Her mother's mouth formed the words: "He'll never accept your brat. The product of incest. An abomination."

Her brain roared. Where is Lucy now? I am the monster. Why did I let myself hide from the memory of her life, my past and let myself drift from day to day, as weeks flowed into years?

Robert had once said he wanted children of his own but I made sure I could never give birth again. I never told him about Lucy or that Little John had been my lover. He only knew that my father's death had thrown the estate into a tangled dispute. Or did he know?

Has Slimmer blown away the shroud? But Slimmer could not have told him how it really was, nobody could. Nobody knows how bright those years were and how much I loved Little John and Lucy. Nobody knows how the pain of looking back has kept me from looking back because the pain of remembering how I felt has kept me from feeling anything at all.

Sara found her mask and reset her features. She tried to smile. She gazed carefully at her husband. She stared down the cruel glint in Slimmer's face and quelled the sea and its waves that crashed inside her.

"What has that to do with me?" she asked

Slimmer huffed.

"With you? My dear, it's all about you. Your family."

She waited, hiding in the silence of her mind.

"Oh, you mean the estate," she murmured. "I forgot about that long ago. They've been arguing about it forever."

She heard her voice fade.

Slimmer's eyes flashed with a kind of joy.

Robert sighed. She was still, at least in appearance, the Sara he knew.

"I understand, I'll handle the details," Slimmer said. "But Sara, you and Robert need to come and see me tomorrow to sign a few things. You know the estate has to be settled and there are papers."

"Yes, papers," she murmured. "I'll stop by tomorrow afternoon after my pottery class. Then I can go to Nordy's."

"Good." Robert said bleakly. "Tomorrow."

Slimmer stood up.

"Tomorrow," Slimmer said. He smiled thinly at Sara. "Then we'll be done with it."

"Yes," she said, nodding and moved out of the room.

Upstairs in her room, the rain still ran down the leaded pane and the faint brightness in the sky was only memory. The dead, cold unreality of her present life gave way to a real pain of guilt and sorrow.

How had Little John known? She felt his breath lift the hair on her neck. Sara opened a drawer in the bedside table. Her notebook and pen came to her hand.

She wrote:

My island smaller grows
The time tides ate my ego up
City seagulls pick my brains
Tighten my chains
And marrow morrow sup...

I'm rhyming, she thought miserably. I'm losing me. His ghost is making me write songs.

She slammed the book shut. She had to leave the mist that encircled her world at the edge of the lawn. I have to go to her. I don't care. I must close this circle, even if it means the end of me as well.

She chuckled bitterly. Robert will be hurt, in quiet good taste of course. But I can't help that. So fucking what.

"So what?" she said aloud.

So, she and Robert had shared a life now ended. It began in the cold and never became warm. She remembered rain freezing on the windows at McGill University library in Montreal. She remembered the long corridor where students smoked, the tunnel under the snow-covered ground between buildings and the library's stacks with dusty nooks stuffed with books.

****

At first, Montreal had been too snowy and too cold. She hung around the edges of crowds of younger students, afraid to make contact. She was sure the others would reject her if they understood what she really was and would turn away. She had abandoned her child. She was a monster.

Sara found refuge in the books and the ideas that floated in the great library. William Blake's painting of the man reaching for the moon crying, "I want, I want," became part of the new identity growing inside her.

She made some friends and met them for wine and bread in steamy bistros. She grew cactus plants on the windowsill of her apartment. One day in the student union cafeteria, a girl from her Shakespeare class introduced her to a tall, gray-haired guest lecturer, a physician called Robert Bradley.

She noticed he was a kind person and soon realized that he had fallen in love with her. She ate with him in expensive restaurants, wore the pearls he gave her and admired his restraint. He asked her so few questions. She wondered if he knew that he must not ask for too much. She knew that if she ever unlocked the part of her brain that held her memories of Little John and Lucy, if she ever spoke about them to him – that process would shatter her, like a rock shatters crystal, and she would be lost to him forever.

He must have known she was hiding something, she realized. Still, he never pried.

She did not love Robert Bradley. But she did not want to love him, or anyone, because love would kill her. Love was poison. She could like and be fond. She could be calm and easy in the dark and drifting snow.

When he asked her to marry her she said she would ask her mother and flew home for a week. The words to "Bye, bye Blackbird" rang in her mind as she boarded the airplane.

Hard was Katy Stone. Harsh was Katy Stone. Dark eyes like coal drills, her mouth a knife edge. That child's father had bad blood. Bad blood.

Of course Sara should marry the rich doctor, must marry the rich doctor. But Sara needed to face facts.

"What does he know about you?" Katy demanded.

Sara shrugged.

"He loves me," she murmured.

Kate snorted.

"Well good for him. I suppose you've got the looks he needs. He's getting on. You're not too bright. It should work. Unless –"

"Unless?" Sara's heart swelled with pain.

"Unless he finds out what a mess you made of your life. Make sure he doesn't find out. He'll drop you like a hot potato. Doctors want prestige in a wife, not a tacky drug-addicted past, an incestuous relationship and a bastard kid."

Sara nodded. Something else began to die inside her. She was surprised. She thought everything was already dead.

"I'll make sure the lawyers keep the kid under wraps. There's no reason for the good doctor to find out anything. That'll be for the best," Katy said.

Sara remembered Katy's hand reaching through the dusk, remembered how hard it felt when it grabbed her shoulder and that her soul froze in its grip.

My soul remained frozen as I wandered through the years of this marriage until now. I was not alive but I could smile carefully. I looked straight ahead, unable to look back and I was thankful for Robert's blind love.

What now? What now?

Sara's fingers traced the rain as the flat glass streaked with rain, bubbles formed, ran together and then sank to the ridge of the window.

What now? What now?

Little John is back in the shape of his letter. His body was dead but now his spirit has come back and somewhere there is Lucy. Where is she?

The casket that had been Sara's soul cracked open and she bent double with pain.

I have to find her, hold her and say goodbye. I have to face her and what I have done to her. Then, maybe, I will join Little John.

After all.

Chapter Fourteen

Downstairs, Robert looked at Slimmer.

"What now?"

Slimmer put the letter back in his briefcase.

"It may make no difference," he said smoothly.

"It depends."

"Depends?"

"On – you know– the course of things."

Robert watched Slimmer pick up his briefcase. "The course of things. Yes. Well, things must take their course. Although, I thought – Sara seemed so –"

Slimmer's eyes flicked down and away.

"It's the rain," he purred. "We've had too much rain. It gets everybody down. She'll get over it."

The lawyer walked from the room, into the lobby, put on his coat, and opened the front door. Robert followed him outside.

Slimmer climbed into his Porsche. He opened the driver's side window and looked up at Robert.

"Let me know if she says anything," Slimmer said before he started the car and closed the window against sleeting rain. The engine roared as the attorney shifted away and down the curved driveway.

"I have never have liked that man," Robert murmured as he cooled his forehead on the nearest pillar. He moved his head sideways and looked at the landscape rolling to the lake in cold gray light. Rain gleamed on the pruned box hedges and on the concrete statues lining the path to the formal gardens.

This side of the lake is another world, he mused. It is connected to the city only by pavement and wire. It is my safe place away from the hospital.

Here, I measure my life in cups of latte and the miles I jog. I am measured by what I own, this home, these gardens and my wife, Sara. She is so fragile and so beautiful. Now, what now? Will she leave me, leave all this?

So far, I've been able to keep her. I have made sure she never hears the moans of the hungry, the cold and the dying. I have kept her from the anguish of the city and the tragedy I see at work. She has been my orchid, rare and precious.

He closed his eyes, trying to stop remembering what he knew; what he had always known. He had never expected her to be passionate because he knew that once her passion had almost destroyed her. He respected her privacy, her secrets. He never told her that he knew all about Little John and Lucy.

He remembered hiring a detective to investigate her soon after they had started dating at McGill University in Montreal. By the time that detective came back with his report on Sara's past, Robert was too much in love to care.

I thought I was so smart, he thought. I was so aware of my money, my family name. Every time I started to get serious about anybody, I had them checked out. I was sure I could avoid future problems that way.

Robert smiled grimly.

And then I met Sara. I would have loved her if she had been a murderer. My heart ached for her. I knew I could not change her past but I thought I could keep her present safe. I thought I could own her, shield her. I thought I could keep her from contacting him, that man who had hurt her so much. I thought I could keep her for me, me alone.

Rain ran into his eyes.

Will she go away now? Will she forgive me? Will she go to find the child? Have I lost her?

The cold stone was hard against his temple. Rain drove sideways across the lawn.

For all these years she has seemed to be content, he thought. And I kept her that way. I thought I kept her that way. It has been enough so far. It has to be enough.

He felt reality slipping away. Dark thoughts and sharp feelings made his eyes sting and his stomach knot.

Mom and Dad were like her, fine, gentle and calm. Everything was so right with them. I wonder what they would say now? Why did they have to die in that car wreck while I was still in medical school?

The wind blew chilly drops into his face.

That was when I entered the ice age, he thought. Where I still live.

He groaned out loud.

Rain drummed the gutters.

The sound turned into the clattering of trays in the student cafeteria. He was back in Montreal.

****

"What would you like?"

The waitress was French Canadian. She was petite, had dark brown hair and alert, brown eyes. Her accent was heavy and her breasts pointed at him through the bib of her white apron.

Robert took in these details with one glance and was amused. This was the first time he had bothered to eat in the student area. Montreal had thousands of great restaurants. But today he had been pressed for time. He had an extra class to prepare and had decided to take a short lunch break.

Something flashed at the edge of his vision.

A tall, golden-haired girl carried her tray to a table. While her steps were firm, there was something sad in the angle of her neck and the way she sank into the seat. Robert's eyes were caught and held. He wondered if the waitress would know her. He heard himself speaking.

"That woman, that one who just came in. Does she come here often?"

The waitress followed his glance across the room.

"Mais sur," the waitress replied with a knowing smile. "She is a student here. She has lunch many days here. Yes?"

"Oh, of course," Robert mumbled.

The girl entered his dreams that night. She entered his thoughts the next morning. Robert returned to the cafeteria at the same time the next day. She wasn't there. He came back the day after that. His heart skipped a beat when he saw that she was there again. She was having lunch with a female student in one of his classes.

As soon as he could, he asked the student to speak with him after class. He described her lunch companion and said he wanted to meet her. He knew his behavior was unethical but this was, after all, French Canada and fraternization with adult students was considered a benign infraction. He was still a young man and enjoyed this more liberal view. His student looked at him speculatively, grinned and agreed to be with Sara in the cafeteria the next day. Her name was Sara Finchley, the student said.

A few days later, after they had lunched as a trio twice, he waited until the friend went to the restroom and asked Sara out for dinner. Sara's eyes scanned him. She shrugged her shoulders and nodded.

He wanted her. She was completely different from the other young women he dated. He bought her wine and dinner and told her that he was from Seattle in Washington State in the United States.

She told him that her family was in Oregon.

He told her that he was in Montreal as a guest lecturer and was working on a research project in geriatric science at McGill University's medical school.

She said she was studying English literature. Her eyes were distant, as if most of her was somewhere else.

He took her to night clubs, plays and symphonies. She was pleasant, placid and uninvolved. Occasionally, when she caught sight of a child, her control waivered and he sensed a deep sadness.

In a basement restaurant on Stanley Street, over steaming bowls of French onion soup, he asked her to marry him. She hesitated and then calmly agreed. He knew marrying him provided her with an alternative to what? He did not let himself think about that. He decided then he would never let her know he had found out about her child and her relationship with her step-brother. He would keep her safe and enclosed.

In his suite at the Queen Elizabeth Hotel, after they finished a bottle of champagne, she told him she did not want a big wedding. Montreal was a lovely town. Perhaps they could be married there, quickly and quietly. She looked at the fat snowflakes dotting the window.

"Anything you want, anything at all," he said, as he led her to the bed.

She responded to his lovemaking with a slight smile and strong automatic physical responses because she was a healthy young woman. At the same time, he knew there were feelings within her he would never be able to reach. He did not care. She was his.

They were married in an Anglican church near the river. They had met the priest, convinced him that they were Episcopalian Americans and had their banns read for three Sundays to a congregation who had no idea who they were.

****

What a strange wedding that was, Robert thought as he watched rain glide over bent grass.

We were so alone. My lawyer was there. Sara did not invite any friends, saying nobody knew her well enough. I felt the same way about my acquaintances. Her family showed up.

He grimaced at the memory. What a gruesome group! Mother Finchley, queen bitch, father hard-faced and frail, brother the blimp, and of course, their lawyer at the time, George Right.

At least I played my part correctly, he thought.

I made sure they saw me as selective and discriminating, with lofty standards. I thought this would keep them from bothering us later. I knew Sara wanted to be as far away from her family as possible. Once she became my wife she could be safe in my world, with me.

She was safe. She has been safe.

She is still my one truly beautiful living possession, even as I age. The skin on her high cheek-boned face remains as taut and smooth as the faces of my porcelain figurines. For all these years she has been cool, calm and mine.

He sighed.

Our pastel world was not passionate, yet she did not complain. I treated her carefully. I was able to satisfy my needs. I think I gave her pleasure.

I let her take English and art classes. I let her go to Mexico, Hawaii or France without me. I asked no questions, even when I wondered if she slept with other men. I am so much older than she is. She is entitled to whatever happiness she finds.

Even now?

Even now. She is established here. Here in my world. She is part of it, although at first the neighbors wondered about her.

All anybody could gather was that her family was based in Oregon and was respectable. I noticed that Sara mentioned her parents only when conversation required it and shared no family details. Our friends understood she had some sort of ongoing dispute with her parents. At the same time, Sara worked hard at being accepted.

Nobody questions us now. She makes the rounds of the lunches, functions and fundraisers with so much dignity that she is a predictable part of the pattern. She is one of us. She is the one perfect thing in my life. My professional life has become of little value.

Depression gripped him. I used to be a real doctor, he thought. Now, I merely keep up with appearances. Once a week, I lead a flock of white-coated interns through the wards at Soundview where the old and indigent come to die.

I look at the charts, nod my approval and then go back to my office where I write papers, talk to my stock broker and deal with selected relatives of my better insured patients.

I know how to tell people that their mother, father, brother or sister have the very best care that I walk the wards and talk to each patient and that after each walk the staff meets to discuss each patient.

I know how to reassure relatives, despite the fact that the patient is most likely to die alone in a curtained cube, drugged and drifting between memories and bouts of unexpressed pain.

That's my work in the twilight world where there is nothing I can do but make adult children feel better with peaceful fiction.

Peaceful fiction. A dream on the edge, like my marriage with Sara. Despite that, I am good at my job. I must be. Their names? My patients' names? What kills them? Death kills them. They have lived out their time so I comfort their children as well as I can.

Thank God it's over every afternoon. Tears ran down his cheeks.

He tried to to think positively. I've reached the peaceful, calm, ordered stage of my life. I earned it.

As rivulents ran off the roof, he realized that the air was calm and he felt no wind. Storm clouds were black mountains in the gray sky.

He went back into the house and went upstairs. Sara's bedroom door was open. She sat in the bay window looking out at the rain.

He sat on the bed and waited for her to noticed him.

"Sara," he said gently. "I have been lying to you."

Her eyes widened.

"You! Lying to me?"

"I've known about your son since before we were married."

"You knew." She shook her head. It couldn't have been. "You said nothing."

"I couldn't. I thought you didn't want me to know. I thought, I thought –"

"What?"

"I thought you would leave me if you realized I had you investigated. I thought you would leave me and go back to him. I thought, maybe, you might tell me on your own, when you were ready. I did not want to break our world."

"This world?"

He was silent for a second. Her tone told him the world was gone. The letter had broken it like a rock through a pane of glass. There was only one way to keep moving on.

"You knew where he was?" she asked.

"Before we were married I found out he had been in Portland but the investigators weren't sure exactly where and needed to look further. But by then I did not want to know. I told them to stop looking."

Back then, she could not have gone to Little John because back then she would have lost Lucy, Sara thought. And she still lost her because back then she thought if Robert knew the truth, he would end the marriage. Without Robert's support, even if she found Lucy, she knew she would have no way to survive. By now, Lucy probably hated her.

Robert and I have always lied to each other, she thought. We are both cowards and have let the years go by unchanged by honesty. Now, a letter has changed everything.

"Where is he now? Where is Lucy?"

"I don't know. I think Slimmer might know where he is. He said that the letter we looked at needed to be discussed. I think Slimmer also knows where Lucy is. Today, he said you and I should come to his office tomorrow. He said he had documents for you to sign. I have a feeling that he thinks you will be more likely to sign them if I was present.

" I want you to go alone. Make him tell you everything he knows about your daughter and her father. You decide what to do. You have the right to know. I think you and your daughter are due an inheritance, enough to support you for the rest of your lives. You won't need me anymore."

His voice was bleak. Sara stepped out of her own pain and felt his. He really does love me, she thought. We have been together a long time. In a twisted way, we have grown together like seedlings forced into the same pot.

"You don't know that," she said gently.

He shut his eyes for a second. Now it was his turn to deny hope. He stood up, smiled grimly and left the room.

Chapter Fifteen

Sara sat nervously in Slimmer's waiting room.

The intercom buzzed.

"He'll see you now," the receptionist said.

Sara rose, crossed the room to a dark mahogany door and pushed it open.

"Why, Sara," Slimmer said as the door slammed shut behind her like a coffin lid. "How nice to see you."

Sara fixed him with a level stare and settled in the brown leather armchair facing the desk. Anybody sitting there ended up below Slimmer's chin level and at a disadvantage. "Really," she said.

"Well, I am glad you stopped by," he said. "Now we can get this business over with."

"Over with," she murmured as she tilted her head and frowned slightly.

Slimmer moved some papers in front of him.

"Well, yes."

She waited.

"I was not prepared to see you in person. Alone, that is, without your husband." he said. "But perhaps this is the best. I assure you, I have your interests at heart."

"You do." Her tone was flat. "Then tell me what happened to my step-brother and how I can contact my daughter."

Slimmer leaned back and placed his fingertips together. He looked at her as if she had suddenly become an unwanted spider.

"I have been informed," he intoned slowly. "Have in fact, verified this information. In fact, can say, without any doubt, about the truth of the information."

"What?"

"Your step-brother died twenty years ago."

She gasped, "You know this for sure?"

"There is no doubt."

"How long have you known? Where did he die?" Her voice rose. The lies were everywhere, nothing was solid. She was drowning.

Slimmer looked away.

"He died here, in Seattle," he said slowly. "In Soundview Hospital. He remained unidentified until recently. A lawyer, Shirley McBride, used the letter I showed you yesterday to track down the death certificate."

"Shirley? The woman who signed his checks when he was at school?"

Slimmer nodded.

"Seems this Shirley McBride could not leave the case alone although she hadn't been assigned to it for years."

Sara felt her mind slipping. It was not Shirley who could not leave Little John alone. Little John had not left Shirley alone, or her.

"How did he die?"

"The medical examiner said it was first assumed to be a drug overdose but the autopsy revealed another substance. A poison, in fact, had been ingested with cocaine."

"When did Little John write the letter?"

"He probably knew he was dying. He was trying to reach his daughter, reach you. The letter indicates he has had only one heir, your daughter, Lucy."

Her eyes flickered as if caught in a breeze.

"So. Where's Lucy?"

Slimmer's eyes glittered back. He remained silent.

Her breath caught and held in her throat.

"Lucy. Where's Lucy?"

Slimmer leaned away from her as if she had some contagious disease.

"Your daughter."

She nodded angrily.

"Where is she? I need to see her." she said.

"I have spoken to your mother and your brother. They feel, and I agree, that for the good of the child, there is no need for her to be involved now, at such a late date."

"Such a late date," she echoed.

He nodded in the still, dark air of the book-lined room as the walls came closer and the ceiling lowered. Sara felt buried alive in the gray, mute air.

"Your father made sure she will be provided for as long as she lives. Your father, your father, believed in family, in familial obligation – to a point."

"Familial obligation."

Sara studied him. He revolted her.

Here it comes, she thought. The clawed hand of Katy and the fat grip of Philip. She decided to let Slimmer finish speaking.

"But there are, as there always are, as you know, limits," Slimmer continued. "The girl does not have to be troubled."

"Of course," Sara said smoothly. " I suppose Robert doesn't need to be troubled either."

Slimmer did not read the expression in her eyes. His tone became more confident, more assured.

"Robert does not have to be troubled either," he said. "Everything can go on as before."

Inside her, her soul like the core of a carousel, began to turn, sending phantom faces spinning past in the darkening room.

"There are of course, papers for you to sign," he said.

"Papers," she said.

"Your mother and brother will give you one-third of the stocks and bank holdings of your father's estate as they were valued at the time of his death, after costs of course, as a lump sum. They will continue to guarantee a good yearly sum for the child as long as she lives and your husband need never know she is your child.

"On your part, you agree not to claim your part of the estate, as dictated by your late father's will, have no contact with your daughter and you agree to the settlement proposed by your mother and brother."

"Where is she?"

Slimmer blinked.

"Your mother? She's in Abraham."

"My daughter. Lucy. I want to see her."

Slimmer's eyebrows clustered over his nose. He cleared his throat.

"I must. I must say that I don't recommend this." His voice creaked a little.

She shrugged.

He went on, pushing urgency into his tone.

"Your daughter was sent away for the purpose of separating her as much as possible – excuse my mentioning it as a matter of business – any reproach and exposure that impends over yourself. I mean, her birth, her birth alone – "

Sara shrugged again.

"Her father was not my real brother," she said. "He was my lover. He was her father. I am her mother. I will see her. It is time to close the circle." she said.

The words were finally spoken. The gates to her soul swung wide.

"Well, Sara." Slimmer murmured, leaning forward again.

"I advise strongly against that. You must know that is a dangerous proceeding. It is unnecessary and will awaken needless speculation – rumor – the press. Your family is prominent. Your husband is well known in his profession. They will find that exposure intolerable.

"Besides, it is a violation of the agreement you made with your family years ago, when you left for Montreal. You agreed to keep things as they were, to keep the child out of the picture, out of this exposure. I must say; I must say. Today you are, and you have been since yesterday, very different from what you were before. Very obviously so!"

"Well," she began. "I feel, I feel –"

He interrupted her.

"Now, Sara. This is a matter of business, your family's business. Feelings come and go but the business of your family and your husband does not. That business depends on the smooth transition from year to year. It is not about you and your feelings now. If feelings were an issue, we would not be here now, having this conversation."

Sara looked at him through a shimmer of tears.

"That's just it, feelings should have been an issue. I haven't let myself care for too long."

Slimmer pushed his chair away from the desk and walked to the window. With his back to her, he stared out of the plate glass. He gave her time to compose herself, as if she were a recalcitrant witness. Then he turned to her. He spoke slowly and clearly.

"You must get over this," he said. "If you go and see your daughter now, she will naturally ask questions. As things are now, she has every right to ask questions. Until you waive your rights to the inheritance, she is an heir to the estate. And even so, she will have rights. But what are rights after all? Rights must be claimed before they really exist, before they are granted.

"Your daughter will not make claims if she knows nothing about these rights. She does not need them. She knows nothing of you or of your new husband. She is living well. She will continue to live well as things are and are planned. But if she meets you, your whole family is compromised, will be compromised. You cannot worry about feelings. Not now, not after all this time."

Sara's eyes flashed.

"I must. That is *my* right. I am claiming it. I must see her again. And, by the way, I am not signing anything. My father's will, as he wrote it, stands. Katy and Philip have been fighting to change it since he died. If they had a chance of succeeding they – you – would not have come up with this offer."

Slimmer frowned. He had underestimated this woman. She was much more aware of what was going on around her than he had thought.

"Now," Sara said firmly. "Where is my daughter?"

Grim-faced, he returned to the desk. He grabbed a pen and piece of paper and wrote down an address. He held the paper out.

"Here," he said. "You are doing this against my advice, very much against my advice."

She stood up and took the paper.

"I know," she said, hunching her shoulders. Her eyes held a hint of triumph.

He looked away.

"Thank you," she said and left the room.

Chapter Sixteen

They kept asking her what day it was. Between sleeping and waking, Lucy tried to remember. Why was it so important to them?

Lucy drifted between a bright, warm place where she was strong and had no pain, and a gray place where her ears roared and she could not see.

It was better where she could look at the waves and the clouds, golden, blowing grass, scraggly trees marching down to the rocks, foam strips in salt air.

Her legs were short and it was hard to climb over the bigger rocks but Mom and Dad were there. They laughed in the bright sun and they laughed when the waves sprayed them and they were all wet. Dad picked her up and she rode high on his shoulders as they bounced along the edge of the water. Mom ran in front jumping up and down, her hair like gold feathers, sparkling with drops. Mom laughed and flung her arms out like a bird. The ground swirled and rippled on either side. Then they were gone and she was falling, falling.

Someone was standing over her.

"Do you know what day it is?"

She looked at the blurry shapes around her. She felt sad. Her mouth was dry and tasted bad. Her head hurt.

"I don't know," she mumbled. "Can I have a drink of water?"

One of the faces came closer.

"We'll see," it said.

Lucy had the feeling that she would have to do something to earn her water. The blurry face seemed to be male. It did not trust her.

"What is your name?" it asked her.

"Lucy," she said.

"Lucy in the Sky with Diamonds" a voice from the dream world sang through her mind.

"Can I have some water?" she asked again.

"I'll send a therapist to see you," the blur said and went away.

Lucy stared at the ceiling. She wanted to go back to dreaming but she couldn't. She realized that she was back in reality. She didn't like it.

She remembered the sun in her eyes, a shadow shape. Had it been a deer? She remembered turning the wheel and flying up in her seat. No wonder her head hurt. She'd hit it on the car roof. She must have totaled the car. Now what. She better call Larry Miller.

The thought faded as she went to sleep again.

Her mother was blowing on the window, making a mist and tracing hearts in the dampness. She took Lucy's finger and drew across the pane, saying as she moved Lucy's finger, writing and saying, "Mom loves Lucy."

The words echoed and faded as Lucy's finger drew the shape of a heart in misty air above her bed. She awoke as her own voice echoed in her mind.

"Mom left Lucy. Mom hates Lucy. There is no Mom."

Lucy heard voices in the hallway outside her room. They were fuzzy and she could not understand what they were saying. It had been like that when she was a baby, she remembered, before the people came and took her away.

She couldn't focus, couldn't stay completely conscious

Scenes from her life floated out of the darkness like paper scraps exploding from a storm drain. Mom and Dad were gone. She tried to remember them and to get them back by going to the sunny day on the beach. But they were gone. They had been gone when the men found her in the closet and took her away. They were still gone when they took her to the Grace School for Girls. They stayed gone.

Lawyer Larry Miller was paid to deal with her, to bail her out of trouble, to keep her fed and sheltered but he would never tell her about her Mom and Dad.

She had asked him about them. He said she shouldn't ask because he could not tell her. It would do no good. But his eyes drifted away in his stiff face. She knew Larry should know something because he had inherited her from Benjy, the first lawyer who used to visit her at school.

Oh Benjy, she thought. Miller would not say what happened to him either but knowing what she knew now, Benjy she figured, would be in jail.

She twisted on the flat, white hospital bed. Her legs ached. She wanted to go home, home to her double-wide in the mountains, home to the wall in the spare room covered with photographs of her friends, mountain skies, dogs, cats and trees. Her wall was her peace, her place. She wanted to go home and back to her wall because something there was in her that loved a wall, her wall.

I have to go get there, she thought. I need to call Larry. He needs to know that I just turned my Honda into scrap metal. They must have called him. Was his number in my purse? She slept.

Dark rain, streaming rain surrounded her. The road disappeared into a fog and she was flying. Why was she flying? There were branches below her. She could see them through the windshield.

Lucy opened her eyes. The light from the window stung. She slept. Mom was soft and all around her, reading to her, making her look at the black shapes on a white pages and repeat the sounds that were the same: mob, bob, dob, sob.

****

She was in her dorm room at Grace, so she sat cross-legged on her bed and told Bravil about how Rudy had cut up the bedspread and the teachers were blaming her, Lucy. She knew she hadn't done it but all the hundrillions looked identical. Bravil was the best of the hundrillions, her one hundred identical twins. Rudy was the bad one.

****

The bald eagle wheeled low against the dark spires of cedar and hemlock, its white beak poised to stab. Lucy leaned her back against a tree trunk and watched. The eagle dove. In a flash it was skyward again. The mouse it carried wriggled in agony and died.

****

Lucy opened her eyes again. A pink face on a short person in a speckled dress stretched into a smile.

Lucy glowered at the face.

"I want to go home," she said.

"Oh not yet," the face said. "You're not ready."

"I want to call my lawyer," Lucy said. "He'll get me out."

The face turned expressionless and stern.

"We've spoken with him," it said. "He left it up to us. Now you wait a little until you are better."

Lucy turned away and went back to sleep. She ignored the voice in the background until it went away. All she needed was sleep and she could do that at home.

Lucy swam to the light and opened her eyes. Faces pushed down around her and shaded the gray window. They were smiling and talking to her. What if? What if Lucy should be dead?

Dead she was not but not alive either, dream-talking and dream-walking, not dead at all. She was alive somewhere else, alive where she was in control and where –

"Lucy?"

"Lucy?"

The voices were insistent and piercing. They pulled her reluctantly from the strong, alive dream world and back to the confusion of other people, things and her feelings of never, never, being right, never being what she was supposed to be, never knowing what she was supposed to be – never –

"Lucy?"

"Lucy?"

The faces became clearer. When she felt their light, she rose easily to meet them because they were good to see. They were the two people who liked her in spite of everything. The faces belonged to Jody and Bill Purcell. Jody's wrapped her big hand around Lucy's fist.

"How you doin' Honey?"

Jody's voice is rough as rock, loud as wind, warm as a wood stove and real as driving rain. Jody's voice brought Lucy to the surface and beached her in the flat, white hospital bed.

"Better," Lucy croaked, trying to smile.

Bill furrowed his already wrinkled brow and looked uncomfortable. Lucy knew he hated driving to the city. He hated hospitals and he never knew what to say to someone who was in a sickbed.

"Jody said we were gonna see you," he said. "And so here we are. And there you are, lookin' sick as a salmon-eating dog. Your face is green as moss."

He turned to Jody.

"Look she's tryin' to smile! That be somethin'!"

"We was in Portland visitin' Mom," Jody said. "You know, she's been sick. And Bill has no work right now, 'cause of the rain and mud."

"Skidder sinks to its axles," Bill interjected.

"So we was in Portland visitin' Mom and we didn't hear about you until we got back yesterday. We came to visit soon as we could. What happened?"

"Saw a deer," Lucy croaked. "Tried to miss. Car went over."

"That's what we heard," Jody said.

"We heard you rolled clear into Bo Pete's pig yard. Took two hours to get you out. You're lucky to be alive, girl. Ya musta gone down hundred feet."

"For sure," Bill confirmed.

Lucy looked at them and tried to nod. There was some kind of plastic tube in her nose and her head wouldn't lift off the pillow.

"I want to go home," she said.

Jody patted her hand.

"I bet you do honey. What does your doctor say?"

"I haven't seen a doctor."

Lucy spoke slowly. One side of her mouth wasn't working properly. It felt numb. Her words seemed to come out slurred.

"Of course you seen a doctor, Honey," Jody said. "Otherwise you wouldn't be here."

Jody's voice was warm and soothing. Her worried eyes looked across at Bill.

"I don't remember," Lucy mumbled.

"We better do somethin' about this," Bill observed, his face drooping until he looked more like a shar-pei than a man. He moved quickly from the room. Lucy's eyes followed his broad back until it disappeared through the doorway. Her head ached so she closed her eyes again. She drifted off feeling the safety of Jody's hand around hers.

Another voice woke her.

"What day is it?"

Who was she?

Who was she?

She didn't know.

The nurse made her open her eyes and her mouth and swallow one of the red pills. Lucy remembered signing a paper about the pills. The nurse had told her that they were a new drug to help people with head injuries and they were being tested on her. They didn't seem to help much. They made her even sleepier and fuzzier.

That morning she had a visitor who stared at her so intently, she was afraid. Did the pills cause hallucinations?

He looked like a doctor. He stood by her bed and look down at her and she felt his eyes push into her, push into her mind.

There was something in the room between them. It swirled and turned like a mandala. She put her hand out to feel its s-shaped edge. She swam through silver, pulled into something long ago, something very sad. She was drawn into the brightness. Then the visitor was gone, vanished into the hall and she was crying.

Who is he?

Perhaps the therapists are his servants, she thought. They want to cage me, tie me down. I cannot heal here in this hospital, with these people and with those red pills fuzzing my brain. I can only heal on the mountain and I have to get there by myself.

Depression swamped her.

I must be by myself because nobody could ever want me or ever love me. I have never been worth that, she thought. People are nice to me because they are good. But I am not good. If they knew me they would not like me.

****

She sat under a tree at Marion's birthday party by a lake. Her classmates played dodge ball on the sloping green grass. She leaned against the craggy bark and watched.

"Come on Lucy! Come on!" the girls cried.

She could not join them. She had a secret that made her different. She had Benjy. She saw him once a month in a little office they kept for visitors. The teachers called him Mr. Rolled.

She was in the first grade when he first came to see her. He told her to call him Benjy and asked her to sit on his lap and talk to him about her week at school. She liked him. She felt warm and loved in his arms.

During the next visit, his fingers slid up her skirt and slipped between her legs. Then his fingers went up her skirt.

Benjy was proud of her. He said she was a woman but she was must not talk about their secret cuddle.

Visits and more visits. She was his little princess.

At night she was filled with sadness and fear. She was lost in the dark. She was afraid to get out of bed to go to the bathroom so she peed where she lay.

"Why do you do that, Lucy?" Miss Glandston, her house mother, asked. "You are too big to do that!"

She couldn't answer. She sucked her thumb and thought of Benjy.

"You must not tell anybody about us," he told her. "If you tell people our secret, we will never, ever, see each other again."

"Like what happened to Mom and Dad?"

"Like that."

****

Lucy ran through a grassy field filled with holes. As she ran, the holes widened and there were snakes underneath the holes, snakes with hissing heads that wanted her. She ran and ran to avoid them. Louder than the hissing, Benjy's voice cried, "Don't tell! Don't tell!".

She knew she was a sinner because at Grace the teachers explained the sins of the flesh and she knew they would hate her for her secret. In Benjy's arms she felt the same fear that froze her heart during Bible study because she knew she was bad. She would go to Hell.

****

Lucy was skiing down a mountain. Trees slipped by in cold silence but she was afraid of what would be there when she stopped so she kept skiing, wavering back and forth between black firs, down into the deepening dark.

Lucy woke up. She was glad to see sunlight streaking through the slats in the blinds.

She looked to the light, white window and remembered, the day when she was in the eighth grade, Miss Glandston had called her into her office and poured more questions over her, questions about Benjy.

Benjy would never see her again, Miss Glandston told her. Benjy had done some things to hurt little girls.

Had he ever hurt her?

Lucy remembered smiling as she thought about the pain in her stomach.

Hurt? No, no he had never hurt. He had made her happy. He loved her. No, no, she told Miss Glandston, Mr. Rolled NEVER had hurt her. Never at all.

Benjy had been right, she told herself. When people love each other, they are not allowed to stay together. First Mom and Dad had disappeared. Now Benjy.

Her next visitor had been another lawyer. He was called Larry Miller. At first she did not like him at all. He was distant, careful and polite.

I like him now, Lucy thought as sat up in her hospital bed. He actually turned to be a nice person. He has gentle eyes. He can get me out of here so I can drive back home to the mountains.

She pressed her buzzer.

Chapter Seventeen

Larry Miller had never been an easy person to like. He wasn't sure he liked himself. Sometimes, he wondered how he been created because he could not imagine his mother in the arms of anyone. His mother was a widow with expressionless blue eyes and silver sculpted curls. His father had been a successful stock broker who stressed himself into death shortly after Larry was born. Larry could not remember his father at all, despite the gold-framed portrait that glared at him from his mother's mantle.

All the same, in the heart of Larry Miller, there was a small green bud that would turn into kindness and compassion. It displayed no evidence of its existence during his early years at the Charles Wright Academy but began to develop at the University of Washington where he lived in a dorm and studied law.

His fellow students noticed that his room was always neat and his bed always made. Larry was as unruffled as his room. His friends found comfort in his calm company.

Larry understood the differences between people that lay deeper than appearances. He focused on his work, did brilliantly academically, passed the bar on his first try and was almost immediately hired by Slimmer and Sadd.

Larry played handball once a week and bought a condominium in the Madrona area, overlooking Seattle. His dedication to details and ethics helped him rise quickly to a partnership and to his role in Lucy's life.

"She needs your oversight," Harold Sadd told him.

Sadd explained that a Portland attorney called Benjamin Rolled had been caught by one of his clients molesting her daughter. The client pressed charges. Police investigated.

The story made the front page of the *Portland Gazette*. Benjamin Rolled was sent to prison and many people stopped doing business with Rolled, Smythe and Right. One of these clients was the Finchley family.

"The Finchleys own most of the north coast of Oregon," Sadd said. "They came to us."

"Why us?" Larry asked. "We're in Washington."

"Finchley's daughter lives in Bellevue. Lucy is her child but the mother has signed a no-contact agreement."

"Why?"

Sadd told Larry the details of the Finchley estate. Various sections were handled by different members of the law firm. Nester Slimmer dealt with Sara and Robert Bradley. He, Harold Sadd, worked with the remaining Finchleys, who still battled to gain control of the estate.

"We are assigning you the child. You will make sure she has what she needs."

Larry Miller never expected to be involved with Lucy in any way other than as the focus of his firm's fiduciary obligation. He was wrong.

Lucy was thirteen years old when he first met her but looked years younger. Her blue eyes glared at him from under pale white eyebrows. Her full lips tightened as she chewed her knuckles. Across the desk from him, she perched on a hard chair like a wary bird. Her bright and angry eyes surprised him.

"How are you?" he asked.

Lucy shrugged and scowled and chewed her thumb's cuticle. Miss Glandston looked serious.

Since the Rolled episode, no girl was ever left alone with a male visitor, no matter what the relationship. It was very possible, the teachers observed, that Rolled had "interfered" with Lucy.

They decided to avoid the subject. It was better to keep silent. If other parents heard about Rolled, word would spread and Grace would lose some of the rich and lonely girls it sheltered.

So after Lucy denied that Rolled did her any harm, the subject was dropped. Instead, the teachers encouraged her interest in photography.

"Very therapeutic," Miss Glandston said.

Lucy had several tense and silent visits with Larry until one day she took her knuckle out of her mouth and asked:

"Do you know what happened to my parents?"

Larry's heart froze.

For the first time he could have helped her, given her something. But he was bound to secrecy, silenced by the client-lawyer gag. He could only shake his head sadly and slowly.

Lucy started to cry then and hiccup. Miss Glandston shifted awkwardly in her chair because this was much too embarrassing. Girls in Grace did not lose emotional control.

"Benjy never told me! Now he's gone too!" Lucy sobbed.

Larry felt the truth come to his throat like vomit but he swallowed it back down. Benjy? he thought. She called that SOB Benjy? A surge of anger almost pushed the words from his lips. It must be true, that old guy had done it, he seethed to himself.

Miss Glandston paled and looked away.

Larry's eyes blurred but he kept shaking his head until Lucy's tears subsided. He stood up and said goodbye. Miss Glandston walked over and patted Lucy's clenched fist, now resting on her knee.

The next visit, Lucy was calmer.

Larry was determined to do the best he could for her. He asked about her other friends. When he found out that parents of one of her friends were the Moores, also clients of his firm, he asked Mr. Moore to play handball with him. He explained the situation and

asked Moore to think about inviting Lucy to come home with his
daughter during the holiday breaks. Moore agreed because his
daughter, Janet, wrote about Lucy in her letters and it was clear the
girls were friends.

Larry talked to Lucy about photography and bought her cameras,
equipment and books on the subject. He watched as Lucy began to
experience happiness.

The Moores owned a cabin near Mount Rainier. Lucy told Larry
that she loved the summer in the mountains when gold and mauve
wildflowers turned hillsides into palettes of color. She said she loved
the winter during the Christmas break when snow rolled like a
diamond carpet to the trees below. She said she had learned to ski,
snowshoe and look at the stars. She laughed when she explained that
an old nightmare of sliding down a snow-covered hill in the
gathering dark had almost gone away.

So Lucy grew as Larry watched. Her progress gave him pleasure.
Lucy became calmer and he saw that she was brilliant, gentle girl,
with a keen sense of humor. He also sensed that she kept feelings of
worthlessness buried inside her. She talked to him about her pictures
and her friendship with Janet as Miss Glandston listened.

She told him she took photographs in her dreams.

"You have many dreams?" he asked.

"Yes," she said. "But now, not all of them are bad."

Chapter Eighteen

Lucy drove slowly out of Seattle. She knew she was still not herself but she had to get away from the hospital and back to the mountain and her friends.

By the time she reached the foothills south of Spanaway, it was pouring.

I'm driving through nothingness as if it is the beginning of my world, Lucy thought. It's as if earth and air and water are one; the air has no light and the earth unstable.

Her right eye, still drooping, forgot to blink. Tears ran unchecked down her cheek. It was still numb. Her broken eardrum roared.

This will get better once I get home, she thought. I know the nurse with the red pills was wrong.

The nurse said the droop would never go away, explaining that after a cracked skull, Lucy would, most likely, never be the same again and would probably have seizures for the rest of her life.

"I haven't had one yet," Lucy said.

"Four out of five head injury cases have them," the nurse replied.

The nurse said Lucy should think about becoming conditioned to a new dependent life and that she would be kept from having seizures by the red pills. She should forget about going home to the mountain. They would take her to a rehabilitation center where she could be monitored and they could see how well these new pills worked.

"Forget! Forget! No I won't!" Lucy's brain roared.

"I am leaving this place," Lucy said. "Now."

"Against Medical Advice!" repeated the nurse, the therapist, and a man in a white suit who looked like a tap dancer.

"Yes," Lucy said. "I have called my lawyer and he is meeting me downstairs."

She would not forget. She would remember.

They brought her something to sign that indicated she understood she was leaving the hospital AMA. She was resisting their treatment. It was not their fault.

When Lucy climbed out of bed, her leg felt stiff and swollen. She had to remember how to straighten it and make a step. She dressed herself and moved slowly from the room. Her wallet was downstairs, the nurse at the desk said, and then ignored her.

Larry had asked Larry to get her another car so she could drive home and she had called Jody and Bill who told her she could stay with them until she was completely recovered.

"I could use the company, honey," Jody had said. "Bill's off in the woods all day."

So, Against Medical Advice, Lucy checked herself out, went downstairs, picked up her wallet and credit cards and waited for Larry Miller in the cafeteria in the hospital lobby. Larry's face crumpled in a funny way when he saw her. They ordered lunch. He looked even more worried when the curry-flavored, chicken-and-pecan salad dribbled out of the paralyzed side of her mouth.

"Are you sure?" he asked. "You don't look that well yet. Why don't you let me drive you there?"

"No," she said. "I won't get better that way. I want a car so I can drive myself home."

He looked at her and seemed to understand. He nodded.

"I'll have them put a cell phone in it. You call if you need help," he said.

It had taken most of the rest of the day to buy the Plymouth van.

"You need a bigger car," Larry said. "It will protect you more." She signed the papers as Larry had the cell phone activated. She refused to spend the night in a hotel.

She wanted to go home.

"It's getting dark," Larry, told her. "It looks like rain."

"I don't care," she said.

****

Headlights behind her reflected in the rearview mirror. They were approaching too fast and they were too close. They made the road ahead invisible. Darkness shimmered in the drops streaming down the windshield.

Suddenly, white light blinded her as another set of high-beam headlights rounded a bend and came straight for her. Lucy gripped the wheel with both hands.

She peered into the drizzle, squinting into the oncoming lights that whipped passed her. The vehicle behind her blinked its lights.

I'm going too slowly, she thought. It's hard to see and it's hard to drive when I am this shaky. But I can do this. I will not have another wreck.

She knew that the driver behind her wanted her to pull over but she could not see the shoulder of the road. She was afraid to pull over, afraid to veer off the road and end up back in hospital or dead.

She saw the deep black of the ditch beside the road. She worried about sliding into it. The driver behind her turned his brights on and off, tailgated her and then backed off. Then she saw a driveway, barely visible, coming up on her right. It looked wide enough for her to get off the road.

She turned on her right blinker and steered to the right as the pursuing truck rushed past, flooding her car with light and spraying mud and water. Then it was gone.

The night gathered around her like water around a stone. She turned her wheels and stepped on the gas. The shoulder gave way and her right front wheel slid over the rain-sodden bank. The van was sideways in the ditch.

I should have listened to Larry and spent the night in a hotel, she thought. She leaned her aching head against her steering wheel. Tears oozed from her eyes. A lump hurt her throat.

"Fuck, fuck, fuck!" she muttered.

She leaned over and groped inside the glove box where Larry had put a flashlight. "Just in case," he had said.

This is definitely the case, she thought miserably as she slithered out of the car and walked around it, shining her light onto the van. The right front fender was crumpled against the wheel.

The vehicle would have to be towed.

"Just my luck, " she said.

She climbed back inside, shivered in her soaked clothes, reached for the cell phone and called the Purcells.

"You won't believe this," she told Bill. "I slid into the ditch on the Canyon Road, about two miles south of La Grande. The front bumper's squished. Can you call a tow truck? Yes, I'll wait in the car."

She hung up, prepared for at least half an hour of cold and wet waiting.

At least the radio worked.

"Be my lover!" La Bouche demanded rhythmically.

Right. There's a line I won't hear for a while. I had a tough enough time keeping a lover when I didn't look like Mike Tyson on a bad day, she thought.

Raindrops on the windshield reflected the darkness outside.

I wonder what Bob's doing now? Did he worry about me when he heard about the wreck?

It is so dark when it rains up here. But when the sun does shine, there can't be any place more beautiful. It's funny how I fell in love with these hills the first time Janet's folks invited me up to their cabin.

It is as if I had always belonged here. I'm glad I didn't go on to college as Larry suggested. Moving up here was a good thing.

I so hated that last year at Grace, all the teachers talking about making choices for the future, telling me what box I should live in for the rest of my life, telling me how to live it, where to live and what for.

I have pictures to take. The light was right up here. Up here, I can carve out the pattern of my life one image at a time.

I can take photographs of the shifting lights and the shapes I see in the sun gold, mist gray, snow silver and shadow blacks. I heal up here as queen of my doublewide trailer.

Larry had helped her buy the doublewide trailer after she selected it from several options shown her by a local realtor. Larry asked her why she didn't want something larger and closer to the town.

"Skate Creek is across the road and I like the trees around it," she remembered telling him. She dozed off and memories became dreams.

****

It's her first evening in her new home. Larry has left and she is unpacked. She is dialing Janet's number. Nobody answers.

It's a warm night, even for July. I need to celebrate. I'm in my new home. She grabs a jacket, climbs into her car and drives to the Cottonwood Tavern in Ashford.

Stars are pinpoints. They feed me energy and power. The passage ahead is marked with shapes I will keep forever. Like a hunter, I scope the territory, watching for tracks and patterns. My eyes are lenses snapping pictures for the memory album.

Snap! Snap! Snap! The barn-like cedar-shake Cottonwood Tavern is in a gray gravel parking lot.

A ridge of snow-capped crags zigzag the sky behind it and another rises from the riverbank across the road. A weathered cedar sign on a brick building beside the tavern swings under a light. It announces "Showers" and "Laundrymat."

Snap! The heavy wooden tavern doors have handles that are thick spiral-carved posts and its "peer-through" windows are of beveled glass.

Snap! A gleaming bar runs the length of the room inside. A black bear pelt hangs above a pinball machine and a dart board. A bobcat hide drapes over the light shade above the pool table.

Snap! The small platform against the far wall has a wooden pine coffin at one end and a jukebox at the other. Snap! Antlered heads of an elk and a moose look down on the platform with glassy eyes.

Snap! The customers have button-on suspenders straining to keep low-slung jeans above stool level. They hunch on barstools under rows of punchboards clipped to a metal line. Pull-tab containers are stacked along the back counter. Glass shelves are overloaded with hunting knives, cans of peanuts, boxed tents, paintings of eagles on black velvet, clocks made out of deer horns, small plastic jars of honey shaped like bears, yellow plush toy rabbits, doll houses, boxes of goldfish crackers, beach towels, T-shirts, fishing poles and backpacks.

Snap! A winner. A happily grinning man, with his Stihl baseball cap on backwards, wins a box of goldfish crackers.

I am noticed as I notice. I place a sweet and friendly smile upon my face and occupy the only empty stool beside the Goldfish Cracker winner.

Snap! I am eyed by the men. Most of them have shoulder-length hair and full, bushy beards. I have always liked that look. They smell of cedar and sweat.

Snap! Men, plump, well-muscled, small to medium size in height.

Snap! The women eye me too, more suspiciously. I keep my smile unwavering and friendly.

Snap! Large women mostly, some giant-sized. All strong and tough, dressed like the men in jeans, shirts and boots but without suspenders.

I order a Bud. The friendly, pregnant bartender introduces herself as Randy.

"You new up here?" she asks me.

I nod. It is credential time. Blue, brown and hazel eyes are pointed my way.

"I just bought a place over at Paradise Meadows," I explain.

"You alone?" Randy asks.

I nod.

"I came up here some summers to visit the Moores," I say, anticipating the next Important Question of Who Do You Know?

"The Moores. They got a cabin over at Nisqually Park?"

I nod.

The Moores are known. People work for them. I am known because I know them.

And that, for a while, is all that I need to join the smoky, beery tribe at the Cottonwood.

Snap! Faces, I meet several Daves, two Georges, four Johns, a Gater, a Silky, a Chris in each sex, and finally, the only Bob.

Snap! Bob's round, pale eyes belong to a right-angled man. His square jaw rises above a thick, bull-like neck. His shoulders flare wide above his barrel chest. His long blond hair flows to thick biceps and over intricate blue tattoos.

Snap! He's a hunk. Does he speak? He grins when he is introduced. His teeth are white, large and even.

The Goldfish cracker winner vacates his stool. The right-angled man moves over beside me. We are shoulder to shoulder, thigh to thigh. I can't move. Is he real? Or is he memo-sex? I should be repulsed. But I'm not.

****

A white light penetrated her eyelids. Lucy woke. Beams lit the car. It has to be the tow truck, she thought. She slid out of the car and stood on the shoulder of the road, waving the flashlight.

In a few minutes, she was in a warm cab as the truck pulled her van around the switchbacks to Jody and Bill's place.

The driver smiled at her. He knew the Purcells.

"Weren't you Bob's old lady? Heard you got into a bad wreck. And now you're in a ditch. You OK?"

"Yup," she nodded.

"You almost died in the last one."

No shit Sherlock, she thought. Her silence kept him silent until he pulled into the Purcell driveway.

"Here we are," he said.

Jody folded Lucy in her arms and took her inside the wood-heated cabin where dry clothes, a whisky-laced hot chocolate and a warm bed closed out the cold, the dark and memory of the stranger she had seen in her hospital room.

****

Mom and Dad were looking for her.

Her mother was holding her and reading her a poem.

"All the night in woe go over valleys deep, while the deserts weep, famished.

Weeping weak, until before their way. A couching lion lay...

They look upon his eyes and wondering behold a spirit armed in gold, on his head a crown, on his shoulders down flowed his golden hair.

Gone was all their care. 'Follow me' he said.

'Weep not for the maid; in my palace deep, Lucy lies asleep.' "

****

A couple of weeks later, Lucy was back in her trailer. Her strength returned quickly as she enjoyed Bill's opinions about everything, Jody's jokes and Jody's Janice Joplin imitation after just a couple of drinks.

Sunlight streamed through the bedroom window. It was close to noon on a warm morning and Lucy was on top of her bed, comfortable in an old T-shirt and jeans. She wiggled her bare feet.

Bill and Jody are real friends, Lucy thought. Janet, on the other hand, was such a good friend in school but was a snob afterwards, especially after I started seeing Bob. Neither Janet nor Bob had come to visit her in hospital. Janet had still not called.

"I hate cities," Bob explained later. "I never go to Seattle."

That car wreck changed me, she thought. My feelings for Bob have changed. Sex with him is not fun any more. That last time, while Bill and Jody were at the tavern, it was not as sweet. The thrill, she decided, with a surge of humor, is gone.

Good thing I healed fast at Bill and Jody's. My head has stopped aching and my face doesn't droop.

Lucy got out of bed, slid her feet into sneakers, and went outside into the warm air.

Rap! Rap! Rap! A woodpecker hammered high in a hemlock.

An engine coughed in the distance and then roared up the hill to her trailer. She went outside and waited on the porch. It was Bob in his old red pickup.

The season has changed, she thought. To all things there is a season. Bob's season as my lover is over but he still is a lot of fun as a friend.

"Hi!" Lucy shouted as the truck sputtered to a stop in the driveway.

"Yo," Bob said. His hair floated in bright strips on a torn black leather coat. The tattoos on his wrists were dark purple.

"Yo," she said.

"Wanna go to the beach?" He asked.

She looked up at a cloudless sky.

"Sure."

She ran back inside, grabbed a jacket, a blanket and a bottle of wine and said:

"Let's go."

Bob was gazing at the tops of the hemlock trees. She wondered what he was thinking about. Bob often stared off into the distance as if he were thinking deeply but never said what about.

Maybe he just stares, she mused. Maybe he can just sort of turn his mind off and wait like a tree.

The truck rattled down the highway. Snap! Brown deer eyes stared at them from a green bank. Lucy sighed. She used to like the taste of venison but she had seen too many sets of those eyes peering at her from the bushes and seen too many soft abandoned bodies by the side of the road.

As they passed the telephone booth in front of the Cottonwood Tavern, they saw Laura Doone crying into the receiver.

Lucy did not know Laura well but she suspected that Bob wanted to get to know her better. Lucy liked what she had seen of the tiny redhead, who always had a smile behind her soft southern accent. Lucy had heard that Laura was going through a major heartbreak since her boyfriend took off for New Mexico. Laura was bereft, left, and the object of every mountain male's attention, particularly Bob's.

Bob pulled his truck up beside the booth.

"Yo!" he said.

Laura's eyes were red and her pale face puffy.

"Hop in!" Bob cried. "We're going to the beach."

A mile broke through Laura's rainy face. She climbed into the truck beside Lucy. Bob pulled a bottle of tequila out of the glove box and uncapped it. They each took a ceremonial swing before he churned on down the road again.

Patches of snow lay like pillows on the dark ridges around the lake. Trees fringed the flat white spots and bristled along the edge of gray craggy rocks.

The grass was thick, green and damp.

Bob folded his legs under him at the edge of the blanket. Lucy lay on her stomach in the middle, facing the cattails spiking the green lapping water. Laura sat cross-legged beside her.

They passed around the tequila and then the wine and they laughed in the pale warm sun. Bob explained how hard it had been for him to get dressed that morning.

"I was so hung over I put both legs in the same pant leg," he told them.

A man, carrying a fishing pole, approached them.

"You live around here?" the man asked.

Bob winked at the girls,

"Yup," he said.

"Where's a good place to fish? I been here since dawn and haven't had a nibble," the tourist said.

Bob waved his tattooed arm towards the far end of the lake.

"Yonder," he said.

The tourist squinted into the sun.

"Down there?"

"Yup. That's where them salmon collect. A guy got a ten pounder just the other day."

"Salmon? Now?"

"Yup," Bob replied solemnly. "Weird, huh."

The tourist picked up his tackle and began to walk around the lake.

Once he was out of sight, Laura hiccupped.

"Jeez, Bob."

Bob stared speculatively after the departing fisherman.

"He's gonna walk that five miles," he observed, sounding impressed.

"But there's no salmon!" Laura crowed. "There can't be!"

Bob pursed his lips.

"You never know," he said. "One of them fish could have jumped up the dam."

"Yeah, right. It's hundreds of feet tall."

"A strong fish," Bob suggested. All three collapsed in giggles.

By the time dusk began to purple the sky, the water was black, the tequila and the wine were gone. The trio was, as Bob observed, noticing the "condition of the condition" they were in.

"Let's go eat," he slurred. "Tavern's got food."

The Cottonwood Tavern was jammed with post-work loggers, builders and retired truck drivers. Pull tabs fluttered, beer foamed and stools tilted. Lucy felt foggy with drink so she sat gingerly on a shaky round stool, leaning on her elbows.

The bartender, John, looked miserable.

"Can I get you something?" he asked sadly.

"Just Pepsi," Lucy replied, gratified by the smile that flashed across his face. She knew he did not drink alcohol and wondered why he worked as a bartender.

John seems to hate his job, she thought. He much prefers to pour Pepsis. I really want a beer but I'm already half drunk and it's still early.

Bob and Laura were playing pool. Lucy watched them in the mirror behind the bar. Bob kept his eyes on Laura's small and firm backside every time she bent over to make a shot.

Smoke eddied around the drinkers at the bar.

They are such great people. They are all so great, Lucy thought fuzzily.

They are different from those snooty girls at Grace and different from Larry-the-lawyer. Although, he can be nice. These guys are so tolerant of each other. They fight and argue and gossip but they stick together like glue. Loving glue.

A small cloud of doubt floated across her azure mood as her mind picked up a buried echo of loneliness and isolation and irritation. Luckily, her slightly drunken spring-like bliss sent the cloud scurrying away so she beamed at the faces in the mirror and beamed at the reflection of the parking lot, where a blue BMW slid into place.

It is been such a nice day, she thought. Beamers come to the mountain when the weather warms. A tall blond woman extracted herself from the front seat and walked through the swinging double doors.

Snap. Lucy watched the woman in the mirror. The woman moved to a corner booth and the air shimmered around her.

Who? Who? Lucy's mind whirled and tried to find somewhere to land.

I know her, she thought. I've seen her. I've dreamed about her. But it can't be. I'm hallucinating. I'm drunk and it's too bad because I was in a really good mood until she walked in.

Lucy turned her stool around so that her back faced the bar.

The woman's eyes slowly scanned the room until they reached Lucy, who was frozen and unable to move. Their eyes met and held.

Lucy's mouth formed a word, an unspoken word with more sound than an ocean's roar.

Her mouth formed a word.

Her mouth formed *the* word.

Mom?

Chapter Nineteen

Philip hunched over the papers on his desk. His chair creaked as he shifted uncomfortably. His eyes burned. There are too many papers, far too many papers, he thought. All because of that bastard. That John.

The money will come in time, in time. I just need to wait. The lawyers are working. I know it will be soon, as soon as I prove the will was wrong. It had to be wrong. There must have been a paper somewhere that proves the old man was not in his right mind. Something is somewhere.

Philip saw a familiar shadow creep across the documents. The ghost who never left his mind took shape.

His mind cried out; logic tried to win. It lost. But who is the third who walks always beside us, myself and the phantom – that other specter who stinks of death?

The sonofabitch is supposed to have died. They told me. They told me. He should not have died. I thought he should.

We did as you asked us, the wraith whispered. We made sure he got the stuff. We sent it to where he was.

Where was he now?

"Oh. Gone. Gone," it said.

"Dead?"

"Maybe dead. Gone."

"Gone where? Gone when?"

It shrugged and sighed and groaned as a rat curried from the corner. There is no death without a body. In the dark shadows of the basement office, Philip hears guitar strings. Philip hears the moan of the blues.

He must have died. When? They need to know. How? They all need to know. That damn aunt sits in the court every day counting agates.

There is a child, maybe other children. Maybe he is not dead. His music is somewhere, she says. Each day she waits.

Dead? When? Other children? Maybe, somewhere in the jungle, a ghost is playing music with other children.

Something thudded against the door to the outside. The phantom and the wraith disappeared. Philip walked up the stairs and opened the door. A bundled *Seattle Post Examiner* lay on the stoop. He picked it up and opened it. The print swam on the page.

Behind him, he heard whispered laughter. They were there, waiting for him. Philip would not turn around.

It was a short piece, written by a young reporter who was clearly excited by the strange story of a musician who had disappeared and now was found, an apparent murder victim.

It reported that records had been found proving the suspicious death of John Finchley Jr., known also as Barefoot John. John Finchley Jr. was the lost heir to a multi-million dollar fortune in investments and real estate.

It reported that although the estate had been diminished by years of legal wrangling involving the firm of Miller, Slimmer and Sadd, the funds were still considerable.

But it was the small dark headline that seared Philip's brain. His fingers trembled as his watery eyes tried to focus, tried to take it in. Monster words bounced around his skull, his mind turned milky by the dark lead and the dead words glowing.

Missing Heir Murdered

Oh now? What now? There would an investigation. Now, after all these years. Why now? Why now? He was old now, tired now, and ready to rest.

The wraith encircled him, flowed around him. Philip felt his blood coagulate and stick in his over-strained arteries. His doctor told him to watch stress. He had bad cholesterol and high blood pressure. The little fat cells had leached from his quivering flesh into his mind and his heart.

Tears oozed between the pouches that held his eyes.

Now, what now? Presumed murdered? How could they tell? That man promised me years ago that nobody would ever know, that a hippie could disappear and everyone would think it was a drug overdose.

Sunbeams pushed through the grated window but the darkness around him held fast. The shadows were long and deep. They filled the room and wrapped his swollen body with cold air. They pulled him to them. Old words, very old words, read somewhere, floated with them.

In this last of meeting places, we grope together, gathered on this beach of the tumid river

The telephone rang. The shadows retreated but not very far. Their friend was on the line.

The voice filled Philip's mouth with dust. It was the same man who had promised he would take care of things years ago.

****

The man had not done well since he last spoke with Philip. The trader in death, bribery, thievery and sex had lost business to smarter and younger disciples of the dark.

Over the years, the man had seen evil using weapons that left its older servants in awe. Small children killed each other with automatic weapons . Perversion rode the cyber highway. Wars were ongoing and causeless. A deadly sexually transmitted plague killed thousands every year, with no cure in sight.

Famine turned millions of babies into skeletons around the world while citizens of the most powerful country spent billions on diets. The four horsemen rode as the planets lined up and the earth shook.

Since the man had arranged for Little John's death, times had been tough. Where Little John chose to die had spoiled an otherwise perfect plan; there was no death without a body. Other plans since then also had gone awry. The man had not been able to reap the material benefits of success. He had been forced to sleep under the freeways and in the tunnel under Union Station, where he was only partially amused by helping fellow transients drink themselves to death. He introducing the diseased to the diseased and sold crank, made from battery acid and arsenic. Although this was the drug of choice for the new age, the man could barely survive on the proceeds because there was too much competition. Everybody was cooking and selling the stuff.

The story about John Finchley Jr.'s supposed murder met the man's eye as he was preparing to place a newspaper over his face so he could take a morning nap. The man sat up, read the article and scrambled to his feet. He shambled to a pay telephone.

That fat son-of-a-bitch would pay, pay, and pay some more to keep word of his deal out of the press. The press was on this now. There was money here.

Oh yes. Oh yes. It was time to talk to the sucker and get some serious money. For sure.

****

The fog rolled up from the flat gray sea and swirled up the dock. It masked the round balloon lights and created a womb of mist. The windows of the Fishermen's Dock Bar and Eatery were blurry yellow squares in the thickening air.

The horses in their stays rested heads down, eyes blinded as their topped-hatted handlers dozed. A crow laughed, hidden on the wire. The dank wet mist muffled the sound. Even the lowing ferry boats sounded distant and far away.

A small twisted figure shambled through the shadow along the boardwalk and slithered down the steps to the lower dock. Darkened tour boats bobbed and rats scuttled into their alleys, *where dead men lost their bones.*

In a short time, a bulky shape sidled along the wall and followed. There were murmured words, a few short ones, and then the words became louder, more persistent.

A door swung open for a second so golden light and laughter escaped. The door closed against the dead wind breathing, rank with rotted fish and seaweed, waves rattled stones and a crow cried a warning.

The bigger shape raised an arm but its twisted companion ducked and moved away. Then there was a splash. Something large and soft smacked against the cement on its way down and was swallowed by the flat black salt water. Then the only sounds were the slapping waves and the quick slither of someone going back up the boardwalk into the cloud-wrapped city.

****

The morning air smelled like seaweed and kelp. The gray-green, foam-topped ripples bounced with silver. It was if the sun celebrated its birth after a night and day of being hidden by fog. The white spires of the city spiked a deep blue sky. Across the water, behind the jagged edge of the southern bay, the mountain was a great diamond triangle. Magnificently alone, she ruled the sky and caught the breath of anyone who looked her way.

It was a rare, clear and warm day, when everybody in the city forgot wetness and grayness and laughed in the golden, glitter air.

A little girl dragged her smiling mother down the steps of the wharf.

"I want to find a sea shell! A sea shell!"

"There are no sea shells here anymore, Tania," her mother said sadly.

"Then a rock, a sea rock! Come on! Come on!"

They paused and looked along the beach below the dock where seawater met land, where bird tracks were tiny arrows in the flat surface, made darker and shinier by its coating of boat fuel.

The mother sighed. Her sad smile quivered beneath the shadows that held her eyes. One day they would go to a real beach, she thought, where the real ocean sang. But this flat, foul-smelling stretch was as far as she could take her child the mornings after she closed the bar. The mother did not sleep much and today, since the sun was out, why sleep? Tania wanted to run along this piece of earth that once had been a beach and Tania did not know anything different.

"Look mom! A whale!"

But it was not a whale on its oil-slick deathbed. It was Philip on his back, a once-white shirt straining over his huge belly. His black coat floated around him like the petals of a dahlia. The flesh of his cheeks flapped bloodless over his sand-filled ears. His body rose up and down with the flat, salt-water swells.

Oh no, this was not a beach or a whale. This was horror. She grabbed her child in her arms and ran up the steps where she put the girl down. She began to scream as her daughter wailed a chorus.

A crow circled as the crowd grew and sirens sang above the screams.

Those were not pearls that were his eyes.

Chapter Twenty

Eyes met and held. Lucy's mouth formed a word.
Formed the word.
Mom.
Sara felt stretched spider web thin across the room.
She knows me. My God, she knows me. Does she hate me? She must hate me. Oh how pretty, how pretty. Oh, this hurts. This hurts.
Lucy was trapped in ice, in fire.
Snap! She hasn't changed. She looks the same. Where has she been? Did she hate me that much? Oh, this hurts. This hurts.
Bob looked at the tall woman crossing the room.
Lucy. What is wrong with Lucy? Does she need protecting? Who is this bitch? That woman is older than she looks.
Their eyes held chains and tears. Lucy stood up, frowned and put shaking fingers to her head. Sara slowly extended a shaking hand. Her stomach churned and clenched. Her heart was exploding, hurting her ribs.
Lucy's mouth formed the word again.
"*Mom?*"
Then she shook her head.
It can't be.
"I'm sorry," Lucy said. "You can't be – You look just like – I've been drinking – I'm sorry."
Lucy's voice faded as she turned away.
"Yes!" Sara ejaculated. "Please! I am!"
Lucy turned back. Suddenly, the dam broke.
Anger, fear, loneliness, dreams, hopes and visions whirled and twisted inside her and formed a throbbing lump in her throat. Her eyes burned. It was hard to breath.
Lucy pushed her palms at the air around her if she were beating down the space between them.

Sara stood very still and waited.

She is going to hit me. She needs to hit me. That's OK.

Lucy's eyes overflowed. Tears streaked down her cheeks.

Bob put his pool cue down and ran to her.

"What the Fuck?" he demanded.

Lucy turned her blind, weeping face to him.

Sara stood still, very still, wanting to hold her, to comfort her, feeling she had lost that right.

Lucy cried out. Her tone was accusing, furious.

"That's her. That's my Mom!"

Bob looked at Sara.

"That true?"

Sara nodded.

"I had to see her," she murmured. "Maybe I shouldn't have come here. But I had to."

Bob moved in closer.

Shit, he thought. Women. They always bring shit like this into the bar.

"You OK?" he asked Lucy

Lucy nodded.

"Yes. I can handle this," she said shakily.

Bob looked at her closely, narrowed his eyes, then appeared to believe her.

"OK." he said. He gave Sara a threatening look, just to be on the safe side.

"I'll talk to you later," he told Lucy.

He went back to the pool table.

Lucy battled for control.

Snap! So much pain! She felt the hurt, not only her own, but flowing from this Mom who swayed like wheat in the wind.

"Can we go outside?" Lucy asked. Her voice sound strange and calm as if someone else were speaking.

Sara nodded.

They walked into the sharp smell of dusk. The shadows were long and mountain peaks were pointed teeth against mauve sky. As they left, players, drinkers and talkers looked down, away from the tangible, piercing feeling surrounding Lucy and Sara.

Lucy gulped. Her mouth was acid.

"Hi – er." she stammered.

Sara looked at Lucy's panic-stiffened face.

She has his eyes, Sara thought. She has his soul in her eyes, but I feel my soul in her shape of mouth and in the set of her chin.

"There is so much – so much –" Sara said.

"Why! Why! Oh Hell!" Lucy cried. "What are you doing here?"

"I had to come." Sara said again. "I am sorry," she tried again. "I am so sorry."

Lucy stared blindly at her mother. Rage made her heart thump and her throat hurt. Rage made her want to take this person, this thing, this Mom, strangle it, end it, stop this moment and go back to the beach and the time before when Mom was a dream.

"Christ!" she cried.

Then she saw something dark and sad in her mother's eyes and it stopped the scream in her soul. The tavern door swung closed behind them. It was quiet. They heard only the rattle of the creek on stones.

Sara swallowed. "I had to come here," she repeated. "Now I don't know what to do."

Snap! Crying eyes.

"In a movie, they would hug," Lucy said.

"Could we? Would you?"

Lucy blinked. She stepped closer and felt herself surrounded, first tentatively, first stiffly and then, gradually, softly and gently – and then both were crying.

They drew apart after a while. They battled for control and won.

We are so much alike, Sara thought. Maybe there's a chance.

She looks like I feel, Lucy thought. Poor thing.

Sara groped for deep words but could only use sounds that came from the shallows.

"So, you live up here?" she said carefully.

Lucy almost giggled. No, she thought insanely. I just fuck up here.

She wanted to scream out questions, shout her dreams. But only sound that came from the surface could take shape.

"Yes," Lucy said. "I like it here."

Sara's mouth stayed tight. She kept the words she wanted to say in check, although they pushed at her aching throat.

Sara put her hand to her throat. Lucy saw white fingers tipped with glistening pink nails and tiny moon crescents at their base.

Lucy looked down at her own bitten cuticles and the small line of dirt that edged the nail on her index finger. She put her index finger in her mouth to chew it clean.

"Can I see it?" Sara asked.

Lucy blinked. "See what?"

"Your home."

Lucy nodded.

"I'll get a six-pack," she said. "I'll be right back."

Lucy went inside the bar as Sara turned to stare at the dark slopes looming against faint stars.

I never felt weirder in my life, Lucy thought as she ordered the beer.

Bob hovered beside her.

"I'm taking my Mom to my house," Lucy said.

"Right on," Bob said.

The lot was turning purple in the fading light as Lucy went outside.

There should be a rainbow, Lucy thought. But the ridges were blue.

"Where's your car?" Sara asked.

"I rode with some friends."

"Will you ride with me?"

Lucy nodded. Oh yes she would, she would; she would.

"You'll have to give me directions."

It's about time, Lucy thought.

She nodded.

"I will. We won't get lost," she said and shook her head. I am saying very dumb things, she thought.

Sara blinked away tears.

"Not this time," she said. "Not ever again."

Sara and Lucy drove in silence up the winding road shadowed by Mount Rainier, white against violet sky.

The smell of cedar kindling, wildflowers and damp earth filled Lucy's trailer as Sara sat at the kitchen table.

Lucy poured her mother a beer.

Sara looked around the room.

"I was just a little older than you when you were born," she said finally

"You left me," Lucy said. "What happened to you and my dad? Nobody would ever tell me." Lucy wondered where all her anger had gone. The words had come out as if they formed a simple question, like "How have you been?" or "How are you doing?"

What is happening to me, Lucy wondered. Why am I so calm? I imagined this so many times. I imagined all the angry things I would say. But now. It is just this.

What is happening?

"I was not allowed to see you. They said – they said –"

Then Sara started to explain, what she had thought, how wrong she had been, how sorry she was. Words fell from Sara's mouth as tears ran from her eyes. Her heart twisted and writhed.

They talked until dawn. At one point, Lucy's anger came to the surface.

"You don't understand! You can't understand! I was all alone!"

Sara sobbed and hugged her. Then they started again.

They wept and consoled each other. Sara accepted Lucy's anger and begged again for forgiveness.

Lucy realized she was not alone, had not been to blame and her anger ebbed. There was still some pain but much was behind them. They saw that a hard but passable road was ahead.

The tears went on through the night until light started replacing the dark.

During the dawn hours, time turned and twisted as Sara told Lucy about Little John, their love, what had happened and the drums in the waves on that far away beach.

Lucy listened to her mother's confession and found her own anger replaced with something else – a new feeling, a sad kind of caring. Was this forgiveness?

Sara was determined to earn her daughter's love. Lucy was determined to let her.

I am not angry, Lucy wondered. Why am I not angry? I cannot be angry. She needs my love now as I have always needed hers. This is a circle put together. There is peace here.

Sara asked Lucy to talk about her life, her thoughts and pains. Lucy told her almost everything, except about her relationship with Benjy. Lucy was not ready to talk about that. Sara sensed there was more and that some things could never been completely exposed. It was enough at this time that her daughter was talking to her.

Then, as sun warmed the new earth, Sara and Lucy walked
outside. Lucy led Sara up a muddy trail until they reached three
cedar totem poles behind an abandoned cabin.

Lucy had discovered the poles during a hike. They had always
seemed magical. Her friends told her to put tobacco before them and
burn sage. She was told they had been carved by an artist who once
lived in the old cabin. He had created poles topped by an owl, an
eagle and a whale to mark three points of the compass. Across the
field, across the river and behind dark spires of trees, the pale
mountain's crown was the fourth.

Sara and Lucy stood before the faded cedar owl, eagle and whale.
Overheard, a hawk soared in an updraft. On the ridge a coyote cried.
The wind whispered in the firs and rumpled the river, sending a
long, low ripple of sound from the mountains to the sea.

****

Lake Washington's waters lapped lazily against the strands of
weed. Pale-green algae stirred. Rain glittered the evenly shorn
blades of grass and slanted up the slope to the big pale house.

Robert Bradley looked at gray water from the bay window in his
study.

Across the room, Nester Slimmer paced and said, "She operated
against my advice. But as it happens, it will be for the best because
her step-brother was found dead."

"How best? How dead?"

"He fell off a dock. Drowned. I came to tell you. They think he
had a heart attack and fell into the water. So, now, we have to
recognize our fiduciary obligations and contact the child. Your wife,
albeit inadvertently, has done that for us."

Robert turned away from the rain-streaked window. His gray
mouth moved.

"The child. Her child. His child," he said. His voice was thin and dry.

"The child, through Sara, now will be awarded her inheritance since the father is also dead. We have proof of that and there were no other children, no proof of other children. " Slimmer went on.

"Both dead." Robert repeated.

Slimmer cleared his throat.

"Both Finchley sons. Yes."

"The child? The girl – Lucy?"

"Sara is staying with her."

Robert sighed. He felt old and tired. Would she come back to me? Why should she?

He realized that he should have said something when he saw Lucy in the hospital, saw the beautiful golden duplicate of his wife, semi-comatose in a metal bed. He knew then Sara would soon find her. He did not know how he had been so sure but there it was. It had happened.

"Sara? How is she?"

"She seems to be fine. She called to tell me she wants to stay with the child for now but will bring her back to Abraham for the funeral on Wednesday."

"She didn't call me."

"She told me you could get in touch with her at this number, her daughter's." Slimmer handed Robert a piece of paper.

"In touch," Robert sighed, putting the note in his pocket. Where they ever in touch? What kind of touch?

"Which funeral?" he asked. "Both are dead. We are all dead." His eyes glistened. His voice shook.

Slimmer's eyebrows rose.

"I believe they will not be going to the step-brother Philip's funeral. Mrs. Finchley was adamant about that. But your wife, her daughter and Audrey Smith will be attending the ceremony for

John Finchley, Junior. I believe they have retrieved his ashes from the medical examiner's office and want to dispose of them in the sea."

Robert's laughter barked. It sounded more like a cry. "Tricky on that coast. It's windy. The dust will blow away. It could blow on them. Dust to dust."

Slimmer gave his client a concerned look.

The man is not himself, he thought. Not at all.

Chapter Twenty-one

Audrey waited in the courthouse lobby and Shirley McBride sat beside her. When it was time, they rose together and entered the courtroom together.

Katy Finchley and Harold Sadd walked in behind them, followed by Robert Bradley. Larry Miller, representing Lucy and Sara, was the last in the procession. Lucy and Sara had decided not to attend.

The group sat in a row on the front bench, stood as the judge entered and sat down again so the proceedings could begin.

Katy Finchley kept her back straight and her head high. As soon as this was over, she would take every dime she had and move to Florida.

Her realtor had told her about a nice place in Miami, on the ocean, but thank heaven, the other ocean. Once everybody was buried, she would go there and never come back. Something like happiness smoothed her frown.

The lawyers recited articles, precedents and findings. The judge looked the papers, looked at his watch and pronounced his verdict, finally closing the Finchley case. Big John Finchley's will was enacted. Sara and Lucy would get their inheritance. At the same time, Katy would get enough to pay for a good life in Miami.

The journalists in the back row took a few notes and left. The Finchleys were old news. There was no scandal here.

Afterwards, Robert called Sara at Lucy's trailer. He spoke carefully, abstractly, not wanting any emotion to stop this contact, not wanting anything he felt to drive her away.

"It's all settled," he said. "You and Lucy will be fine. Your mother is packing for Miami. She's moving there after Philip's funeral. I don't think she'll be back."

"Did they ever find out who killed John?"

"No. I guess, even in death, he is an open case." His voice was tentative, hiding a question he could not ask.

Sara understood there was more he wanted to say and more that she needed to say.

"Yes," she said.

"Will I see you in Abraham?."

She heard the pain in his voice. It hurt her too. She knew then she would be there to listen to him when the time was right, just not yet.

"Yes. Take care," she said.

****

Three days later, Katy Finchley wondered why she felt nothing as she sat in the front row of the Abraham Baptist Church. Reverend Tim Bosworth was talking about how hard Philip worked for the community and kept so many people employed. When he asked for others to share memories of her son, only a plant foreman and his maid stood up.

Reverend Bosworth asked Katy if she wanted to speak; she shook her head. She could not think of anything to say. The people in the church nodded understandingly. It was clear to them that she was overcome with emotion.

Did she miss her son? Did she miss her husband? She didn't think she did. It was all over and done with. She was glad that Sara had asked Robert to work with Finchley Incorporated's board of directors to find somebody to take Philip's place as CEO. Philip hadn't done much in that job anyway these last few years, she thought. The managers pretty much run things on their own. It will be nice in Miami. I am sick of this place. It rains too much.

Local residents who remembered the days when Big John was still alive filled the back pews of the church. They would not have missed this funeral for the world.

It was the end of an era. Mitch and Salty sat beside each other. Years of alcohol abuse had pickled the pair but they could still walk and talk, after a fashion.

"That Katy is still an ornery old bird," Salty whispered to Mitch.

"Salt of the old Stone, Mitch whispered back.

Realtors, insurance salesmen, building contractors and lawyers who had done business with Philip were in the front pews. They had hoped to establish relationships with the new heiresses, Sara and Lucy, both of whom were rumored to be very good-looking. The younger insurance salesmen wondered if Lucy could be talked into marriage. They were disappointed because neither Sara nor Lucy were at the service.

****

Sara and Lucy stood on the cliff overlooking Abraham's shoreline where clusters of condos, expensive houses, restaurants, hotels and parking lots were edged by blowing sand. Crows skittered between tire tracks and beer cans. The buildings farthest from the sea were several stories tall as if they were standing on tiptoe to get a glimpse of the surf. Warning signs lined the roads that went straight to the flat, black beach.

Sara told Lucy how about it had looked when she was a girl.

"There were no houses there. It washed clean with each tide and you could find sand dollars everywhere. Sandpipers left tracks on the sand. Rocks covered parts of the beach and you could hide in hollowed-out drift logs when it started to rain. When your father played his guitar, the waves were the rhythm section, providing a kind of rolling beat."

The clouds lay in dark layers on the horizon. Above them, the sun sent flat gold strips across slate gray sea.

Sara and Lucy heard someone coming up the trail. Aunt Audrey and Shirley struggled up the hill. Shirley was panting and carrying a portable tape player in one hand as she helped Audrey up the slope with the other.

"What's in there?" Lucy asked, once Shirley set the player on the ground and mopped the sweat from her forehead.

"Cory had some of your Dad's reel-to-reel tapes. This was your Dad's favorite. I had it made into a cassette so we could play it." Shirley said.

Shirley pushed a button. They heard the harmonics from Little John's guitar. They heard the chimes of the first song he ever played. The notes made Lucy's eyes fill with tears because now she remembered his music. They had sung the song together when she was small enough to ride on his shoulders. Sara began to sing the chorus, taking her daughter's hand.

"If you go down to the woods today, you better go in disguise!
If you go down to the woods today, you're in for big surprise!
For every bear that ever there was, is gathered there for certain
because... today's the day the teddy bears have their picnic!"

The notes were the lilting refrain of a joy almost forgotten, an innocence almost lost.

As the sun set over Abraham, the four women danced in a circle above the blue and beaten sea. Lucy, Sara, Audrey and Shirley became vision and word, hope and reason as dying light hid twisted trees.

When they were done, Sara tried to dump the ashes over the cliff. But as Robert had foretold, the wind blew and the women were dusted by the powder that had been Little John. His heavier remains

buried themselves in the coarse grass. The women laughed at the
perfection of the accident.

Then they walked back down the trail with Little John's notes
still ringing in their ears.

From the parking lot below the bluff, Larry Miller saw Lucy
striding down the path with her blond hair flying like angel wings
behind her luminescent head and he forgot to breathe for a moment.

She smiled at him. His breath came back with a gasp when he
saw the bright gleam of her eyes. She had never seemed so at peace,
so happy.

He suddenly realized that he wanted to hold her but could not. So
he stood without moving, his throat constricted. He would wait. He
could wait. It would happen.

"Hi," he said.

"Hi," she grinned.

"Hey Luce!" shouted a male voice from behind them. Bob and
Laura were in the back seat of Jody and Bill's old Ford Granada.
Jody and Bill were in the front. The windows were rolled down and
all four heads leaned in her direction, smiling.

Lucy turned away from Larry and approached her friends.

"You heading home?" she asked.

Bob grinned, revealing the friendly gap in his teeth.

"Yeah. But first we're gonna check out summa them Indian
casinos on the way. Wanna come?"

Lucy shook her head. "Mom and me are going out to eat. Then I
think we want to go straight home – my home. We still have more
talking to do."

Jody nodded approvingly.

"Told ya," she said to the others.

Lucy waved at them as the old car sputtered and roared inland,
away from the sea to the hills.

Lucy turned to watch Sara who was walking slowly and tentatively towards Robert.

My God, thought Lucy. That's the man! That's the man who stood over me at the hospital!

Robert's gaze was riveted on his wife. His hands shook slightly so he buried them in the pockets of his raincoat.

Sara looked at his pale gray face and thought how kind he looked and how sad. There are bridges to mend here, she thought. The fact that he is here is good. He did not send Slimmer with divorce papers. She understood that he had never really known her and she had never really known him. Perhaps, now, they could start learning.

"I'm glad to see you," she said sincerely.

He nodded and shadows fell from his face. But there was still a question in his eyes, a hard question.

"Will you come home?" he asked.

Perhaps he knew her more than she knew, Sara thought. Perhaps she knew him better than he guessed.

"After a little while," she replied and smiled.

Her eyes were in the smile and his heart soared.

"Lucy would be welcome. She could always –" he said and Sara realized that he meant it. Another barrier between them was gone. He loved her very much. She knew that now.

"You're sure you wouldn't mind?"

Robert's eyes shifted sideways and back.

"I might have a few years ago," he said. "I think you knew that. Now, I would like it. And – I miss you. I think I could, perhaps, make things easier for her and you."

His lids fell. He looked for a moment like an owl, settling for sleep, waiting for moonrise.

She touched his shoulder.

"Perhaps you can. But first, I have to get a little closer to her and let her get closer to me. You understand? Then. Well then. Maybe. She might be willing to come home with me."

Robert nodded.

"She might," he said.

"Or she might want to stay where she is. Either way it's up to her."

"And you."

"Yes."

"You?'

Sara smiled.

"I will have to come home again," she said. "I miss you too."

Robert felt tears as joy caught in his throat.

"I'll be waiting."

Sara turned to where Lucy stood smiling. Mother and daughter walked towards Sara's blue BMW. Larry and Robert watched them go.

"I will keep an eye on them" Larry told Robert before he went to his car.

"I am sure you will," Robert replied. He had seen the look on Larry's face as Lucy walked away.

Shirley took Audrey to where Sandy waited patiently by an old truck. Sandy's eyes were sad and kind. She remembered Little John and felt she owed him something. While Mitch went to the Finchley funeral in the church, she had decided to stay with Audrey.

"Will you take her home?" Shirley asked Sandy.

"I most certainly will," Sandy said. "Us old girls gotta stick together."

Audrey looked gratefully at Shirley and grasped her hand.

"Thank you so much," she whispered. "That boy's spirit is free now."

"I know," Shirley said.

Sandy helped Audrey into the truck and drove away.

"Well?" asked Phyllis as Shirley climbed behind the wheel of Griselda.

Shirley grinned at her friend.

"I'm starved. Let's find a restaurant," Shirley said.

****

Audrey, feeling peaceful and happy, climbed into her bed. It has been a good day, she thought. In the end, it is all good.

****

She was walking slowly down a long hallway. She was met by a small, dark-haired boy whose eyes were full of dreams and starlight.

She knew he loved music, colored stones and his Aunt Audrey.

"Let's go, Little John," Audrey said. "I'd like to hear those Sousa marches. Let's go and listen to them. Perhaps you can play along with them."

"Sweet!" the boy said.

He took her hand and led her gently home.

Gary was waiting for her.

www.ingramcontent.com/pod-product-compliance
Lightning Source LLC
Chambersburg PA
CBHW070102260626
47160CB00004B/1288